You Belong to Me

(Pine Grove Novel, Book 4)

Jean C. Joachim

Moonlight Books

Dedication

To Pop, who handled his disability as if it didn't exist.

Acknowledgment

Thank you to my editor, Laura Garland, and my line editor, Nan Sipe. A special "thank you" to Vicki Locey, and Roz Lee whose encouragement keeps me on track. Thank you to the Joachim men, Larry, David & Steve, and the newest member of our family, Pam, for keeping me grounded and believing in me.

ABOUT THE E-BOOK YOU HAVE PUR-CHASED: Your non-refundable purchase of this e-book allows you to only ONE LEGAL copy for your own personal reading on your own personal computer or device. **You do not have resell or distribution rights without the prior written permission of both the publisher and the copyright owner of this book.** This book cannot be copied in any format, sold, or otherwise transferred from your computer to another through upload to a file sharing peer to peer program, for free or for a fee, or as a prize in any contest. Such action is illegal and in violation of the U.S. Copyright Law. Distribution of this e-book, in whole or in part, online, offline, in print or in any way or any other method currently known or yet to be invented, is forbidden. If you do not want this book anymore, you must delete it from your computer.

WARNING: The unauthorized reproduction or distribution of this copyrighted work is illegal. Criminal copyright infringement, including infringement without monetary gain, is investigated by the FBI and is punishable by up to 5 years in federal prison and a fine of $250,000.

You Belong to Me
Copyright © 2019 Jean C. Joachim
Edited by Laura Garland
Line editor – Nan Sipe
Cover design – Dawne Dominique, Dusk to Dawn designs

ALL RIGHTS RESERVED: This literary work may not be reproduced or transmitted in any form or by any means, including electronic or photographic reproduction, in whole or in part, without express written permission. All characters and events in this book are fictitious. Any resemblance to actual persons living or dead is strictly coincidental.

PUBLISHER
Moonlight Books

Chapter One

D*ecember*

"Look, Dad!" Bobby Morrison yelled from the living room.

Holding a mug of coffee, the boy's father, Cal, strolled into the room and peered out the window.

"Someone's moving in," Cal said.

"Look! A big truck," exclaimed the boy.

Cal chuckled and rubbed his son's head as they watched the men unloading furniture and carting it into the house.

"Go get dressed. School today." Cal shooed Bobby away.

Curiosity riveted the older Morrison to the window. A woman appeared at the door to the small house. Her short, dark hair and the way she moved caught his eye.

"What's she doing here? She's not moving into that house, is she?" he said to himself.

A frown drew the corners of his mouth down. His brows knitted, and anger tightened his chest. Hadn't Giselle Davenport done enough harm? She didn't belong here anymore. Why had she come back? It sure wasn't because of him. Why hadn't she stayed in Europe, where she belonged?

He had a life in Pine Grove now. Her return would spoil things. He'd been over Giselle since the moment she left, or at least that was what he told himself. He'd found someone else, married, and had a child. So, why didn't Giselle stay in another corner of the world?

Drawn to her against his will, he stood there, transfixed, as the burly men hauled tables, chairs, and boxes inside.

"She can't own the place. No. She must be renting. Probably only a brief stop on her way to Timbuktu for another fancy job," he muttered to himself. And maybe breaking another heart? At least this time, it wouldn't be his.

He watched her cling to the wrought iron bannister on the front steps. Frost from the night before made the concrete stairs slippery. Dressed in a short jacket, she wrapped her free arm around her waist.

"She never did know how to dress for winter," he mumbled to himself.

In his head, he listed a dozen things he should be doing, but Cal couldn't break his fascination with the scene unfolding across the street. He'd heard through the grapevine—the grapevine being his mother—Giselle had sold her family's enormous Victorian home. He wondered how she'd get a giant house full of furniture into the tiny two-bedroom job.

Anger grew to bitterness. Why did Giselle have to come back? He'd been doing fine without her for the past six years. He had a life—almost a life. He had his son, their cozy little house, perfect for the two of them, and work with his father. He had everything he needed, right?

Wrong. Since his wife drowned in the Delaware, Cal hadn't had a woman in his life. Jane had been reckless, ignoring his warning about the treacherous river. She'd been swept away by the strong current and smashed into a large rock. Unconscious, she'd fallen below the water and drowned before Cal could get to her.

Since then, his life had been laid out for him—work and taking care of his son. His parents helped out. Every week, Cal and Bobby shared Sunday dinner with his folks. Bobby looked forward to playing with Grandpa, and Cal enjoyed his mother's cooking.

He'd settled into a comfortable routine, and now this—Giselle Davenport moving in across the street. The last thing he needed was her waltzing back into his life. Sure, he'd been crazy in love with her when she left to have a year working abroad. "A once-in-a-lifetime opportunity. Only for a year," she'd assured him. Baloney! He knew different. Once she got a taste of Europe, she'd never come home.

They had agreed to date others during the year. Giselle had frowned when he'd suggested it but went along anyway. Who knew he'd be the first to find someone else? In his mind, Jane had only been a temporary fix. Things between them progressed faster than he'd wanted, and Jane became pregnant. So they married.

The night before his wedding, pain had stabbed Cal's heart. While he did care for Jane, he still loved Giselle. Cal stepped up and did the responsible thing. While his marriage never satisfied him, deep inside, it had worked, more or less. Though he'd lost Jane, he had Bobby, an energetic, curious, exuberant force in his life. Cal adored his son, grateful to have him.

He rubbed his chin as he stared at her place. What did Giselle think? That they'd simply patch things up and start dating again? No way! She was a spider who'd hurt him beyond anything he could have imagined. She'd be lucky to get the time of day from him.

"Come on, Dad," Bobby said, standing by the front door.

Leaving his reminiscences behind, Cal threw on a jacket and took his son by the hand. Their snug house was two streets away from Pine Grove Elementary. They'd bought the house because it was an easy walk to Bobby's school. Having spent yesterday shoveling, Cal made sure their walkway was snow and ice-free, safe for his son.

As they strolled along, Bobby sang "Jingle Bells." Cal shot one glance over his shoulder before turning down the street.

"You like the big truck, too?" his son asked.

"Yeah. It sure is huge," Cal lied, quietly chastising himself for not telling the truth. No reason to tell Bobby anything about Giselle.

When he looked over, their eyes met. She lowered hers first and turned away. *Be embarrassed. You've got plenty to feel guilty about, Ms. Davenport.* So, she couldn't meet his stare? Well, good. It simply meant he wouldn't have to bother with her.

"Come on, Dad. Sing. It's almost Christmas."

Cal joined in. Bobby's ebullience raised his spirits. The child had no idea how many times his cheerfulness had saved Cal's mood. The boy had been depressed for months after his mother's death. At two, he didn't understand and had adapted to having only his father and grandparents. Cal's mother, Betty, stood in for Jane as much as possible.

There were times when Cal's patience stretched from New York to California. The boy's energy never seemed to give out, except five minutes before bedtime. Between being mother and father to his son and working in the tree and lawn business with his dad, Cal ended up exhausted by the end of the day. Consequently, his celibate lifestyle didn't present much of a problem.

Now that Bobby had entered kindergarten, Cal admitted the time had come to find a new wife. While he and Jane hadn't always gotten along, he missed living with a woman, sharing a bed, meals, and decisions about Bobby.

However, in a small town, there weren't many options, and with a child...well, being a father closed him off to women who didn't want the burden. With the arrival of winter, the tree and lawn business ground to a halt. Both Cal and his father had more free time than they could fill. Cal planned to make a list of indoor projects to accomplish while the weather was too rough to work outside.

He kissed his son goodbye and ambled toward home. At Giselle's, there were only a few boxes left. The back of the truck was closed. Cal watched.

A man approached her with a piece of paper and a pen. She brought the paper right up to her face before scribbling something. Hmm, he didn't remember her being so nearsighted. She must have left her glasses inside. But he didn't recollect her wearing glasses, either. He shrugged it off. Things changed over time, he figured.

As he got to the place where their paths paralleled each other, he stopped. After the massive truck pulled out of her driveway, he faced her.

"You're back?" he called out, narrowing his eyes.

She gave him a half smile and made her way down the walk. Halfway there, she stepped on an icy patch, slid, and fell hard on her butt.

"Ouch!" she blurted out.

Cal was by her side in a second. He grabbed her elbow and yanked her to her feet.

"You hurt?" He raised his hand to clean off her bottom but stopped in the nick of time.

Brushing off her pants, she shook her head. "Thanks." She moved out of his grasp.

"What are you doing here?" Cal struggled to keep belligerence out of his voice but failed.

"In Pine Grove? It's my hometown. I've always lived here."

"Okay, then. On Pond Road? Right across the street from me?" His folded his arms across his chest.

"It wasn't intentional. I needed a ranch. Small. Julia picked it out for me before I got back."

"Oh? Julia? And she didn't know I lived here?"

"I guess not. I think it was the only small ranch on the market."

"What do you need a ranch for? What's wrong with your father's Victorian?"

"None of your business." She pushed by him. "Thanks for the neighborly welcome," she sniffed.

"I did help you up," he said.

"And I thanked you. I could have gotten up by myself."

"But you didn't need to, did you?"

She whirled around and faced him. "What do you want? A medal? Should I call the newspaper? You did something neighborly and nice, but don't ask me to give you a Purple Heart." Giselle raised her chin for a second then turned and continued on her way.

He stood, frozen in place, watching her walk away. She still had that haughty sway, the I'm-better-than-you swing of her hips he'd so admired six years ago. Today, it simply appeared condescending and stuck-up.

At the stairs, she slipped again and went right down on the step. From where he stood, it appeared her shin landed right on the edge of the flagstone. She uttered a cry of pain and stopped. Her shoulders heaved once.

"Well, I suppose you can get up from that one on your own," he said, his tone meaner than he'd intended.

"Damn right," she called over her shoulder. But, for several minutes, she clutched the railing with one hand, and her leg with the other.

Cal gave in, strode over, and slid his hand under her elbow.

"I've got it." She attempted to wiggle out of his grasp.

"No, you don't. Why don't you shut up and let me help you?" He eased her to her feet. She leaned against him for a moment.

"Thanks. I've got it," she choked out, staring straight ahead and gripping the bannister.

"Then I'll mosey on home." He moved away from her property, his gaze glued to her back. Slowing his pace, he waited for her to move. Finally, she limped up the steps and fiddled around at the lock. Boy, she'd sure gotten clumsy since he'd last seen her. He shook his head and continued on his way home.

GISELLE OPENED THE lock and fell into the house. She dragged her injured leg across the threshold and slammed the door before nosy Cal Morrison could snoop around. The pain was excruciating. She lay on the floor, hugging her leg to her chest. She felt along the shin bone.

A bump was forming and something was wet. Blood. Crap! She'd cut herself.

Within a minute, shock set in and the pain subsided. She pushed to her feet, clinging to the doorjamb. Tears stung behind her eyes and wouldn't be stopped.

"Damn it." Anger gathered in her chest. "Stop feeling sorry for yourself," she ordered. Sniffling, she limped over to the coffee table, banged into it, cursed, and found the tissue box. Plopping down on the sofa, she grabbed a flashlight from the coffee table and rolled up her pants leg. After examining the gash, she returned the flashlight to the table and hobbled to the bathroom. Giselle kept flashlights, magnifying glasses, and binocs in every room so she didn't have to hunt for them.

Boxes got in her way, especially small ones hiding in the shadows. She bumped into furniture not yet put in place. Negotiating a chaotic house challenged Giselle.

After washing her cut and dressing it, she headed to the living room. Holding the binoculars, Giselle stood at the window. She could make out the Christmas tree in the house across the street. Her poor vision prevented her from distinguishing who moved around. She guessed it was Cal. She had watched him and his son make their way through the snowy streets to school. Pain had pierced her heart. The boy should have been her son with him. She sighed.

"You'd think after dealing with this crap for three years, I'd be used to it by now," she said to herself. Early onset macular degeneration had disrupted her life, robbed her of her profession, and forced her to sell her family home. Her central vision, while not completely gone, had settled in as fuzzy. If she magnified things to huge and the light was right, she could read. Doctors treating her with vitamins and a special diet had arrested the disease, stabilizing her sight.

Giselle couldn't read a regular book without intense concentration, magnification, and bright light. She'd given up on the television and turned her leisure time to the radio.

She made her way to the kitchen and plugged in the electric kettle. The beauty of it was it stopped boiling and kept the water hot with no open fire or hot burner. With help from her aunt, she'd laid out the kitchen and memorized it before the movers arrived.

Find the tea? Easy peasy, she went right to the correct cabinet. Sugar? Milk? Giselle pulled things together for a hot cuppa to chase the winter chill away.

Aunt Julia had picked out this house, a two-bedroom ranch. Though her worsening vision seemed to have plateaued, Giselle couldn't handle stairs. Had Julia known this house was across the street from Cal's? Maybe not.

Whether she wanted it or not, there would be no reunion. Between their anger and her disability, the gap between them was as wide as the Atlantic Ocean. Giselle's plate was full to overflowing, simply figuring out the next steps in her life. Living on her savings, disability, and the money from the sale of her family's home would do for now, but she needed a steady income.

She had instructed her aunt to tell no one about her condition, especially not Cal Morrison. She could take his hostility but never his pity.

Julia said rumor had it, he'd never forgiven Giselle for taking the job in Europe. She'd thought she told him it was only for a year but guessed he hadn't listened. Within nine months of her leaving, he'd married. Devastated, Giselle had cried for weeks, moping around her lovely flat in Paris. To this day, she didn't understand. If Cal had loved her as much as he had professed, he wouldn't have married someone else. And surely not so fast?

After her tears abated, anger and resentment grew in her chest. Cal had been lying all along, hadn't he? He'd never loved her, not really. The moment she was gone, he'd found another woman and didn't waste a second before tying the knot. He wasn't exactly crying his eyes out over her, was he?

She sat on the sofa with her cup of tea. Julia would be by later this afternoon to help her arrange the furniture. In the meantime, Giselle picked up her phone, shone the small, bright flashlight she kept in her pocket on it, and turned on an audio book. She stretched out on the couch, resting her head on one end and her feet on the other, and listened to a romance novel. She loved the happy endings. The mellifluous voice of the narrator soothed her, and soon she'd fallen asleep.

CAL PULLED BACK THE drapes. Since she had no curtains yet, he looked right inside Giselle's house. Watching her bump into things and limp across the room, Cal rubbed his face. She'd never been a big drinker, yet she appeared drunk. He wondered for a moment, shrugged, and then checked his watch.

With the arrival of winter, work for Morrison's Tree and Lawn Care switched from trees to snowplowing. He and his dad had invested in a plow attachment for their pickup, and it had paid off. Cal had plowed at least a dozen driveways already this week. Although no fan of the icy wind that whipped through Pine Grove every winter, he welcomed the work that came with snow. Sure beat being idle.

Bobby would be in school for another hour. Cal had time to breeze over to The Cozy Café and pick up a cup of their fine coffee and a cinnamon bun, and maybe a little gossip, too. He pulled out of the driveway and headed for tiny downtown Pine Grove.

"Howdy, Cal," Laura Dailey said as she wiped down the counter with a damp rag.

"Hey, Laura."

"Coffee and a hot cinnamon bun?"

"How'd you guess?" He grinned.

Laura headed for the coffeepot. "Newspaper, too?"

"Nope. Any local news?" He hoped he wasn't being too obvious.

"Can't think of anything. Oh! Wait. Yeah. Jess and Stryker are having a kids' Christmas party at the inn."

"Nice. That's all?" he prodded.

"Gonna bring Bobby?"

"Might. Nothing else?"

Laura set down his mug and stopped. "Can't think of anything," she said, scooping his sweet bun out of the oven.

"I hear Giselle Davenport's come back," he said, hiding his exasperation.

"Oh yeah. But that's not new." Laura put the warm bun in front of him. "Butter?"

He nodded. "Not new?" His mouth watered in anticipation of the luscious pastry.

"Nope. Rumor had it she'd be returning six months ago."

"But she's just arrived?"

"Nope. Been stayin' with her aunt Julia."

"Six months? Really?"

"Yep."

"How come I haven't seen her?" he asked.

Laura narrowed her eyes and shot a shrewd glance his way. "Maybe because she didn't want you to."

He gulped a mouthful of coffee and contemplated her answer.

"She's been working in that dilapidated thrift place, too. She fixed it up some. Had it open for a day or two a week."

"Really? I had no idea."

"Take your head outta your behind, Cal, and you might know what's going on."

"What did she come back for?" he asked, unable to stop himself.

"Probably not to see you. I dunno. Sold her folks' house. Bought a new place in the flats somewhere, I heard."

"Yeah, across the street from me," Cal volunteered.

"Oh really?" Laura's eyebrows shot up. "Interesting."

"That's why I'm askin'."

"Wouldn't have expected she'd land there," Laura said.

"Me, neither."

"Aren't you the lucky one? To have such a nice, pretty lady right across the street. Mighty convenient, I'd say," Laura said with a laugh.

Cal raised his palm. "Wait a minute. I didn't ask her to move there. And I'm not happy about it."

"Why not? Giselle is a sweetheart." Laura carted menus to new patrons and took their orders.

Sure, Giselle used to be a sweetheart, until she left. Cal's mind dialed back to the last week of the summer. He and Giselle had taken a midnight swim in Cedar Lake. They sat on the dock, dangling their feet in the water. He heard their conversation in his head as if it were yesterday.

"When you comin' back?" he'd asked.

"I haven't even left yet!"

"I know. But I'll be crossing off the days until you get back. So how many days do I have to x off?" he'd asked.

"The contract is only for a year."

"Really? Can they renew?"

"I don't know. It's a long way off. I figure a year in Europe'll be plenty."

"You'll be here next summer?"

She'd reached over and combed his hair out of his eyes. Gazing directly at him, she'd smiled that gentle smile of hers. "I'll miss you every hour of every day, Cal."

The air had stilled around them. Cal leaned over to kiss her. He cupped her cheek and ran his thumb over the outline of her upper lip. "No, you won't. You'll have all of France at your feet. Those Frenchmen. Ooh la la!"

She'd laughed. "Don't be silly. You're the one I want. The only one."

"Yeah? Tell them that."

"There won't be any 'them.' Only you. Can you wait?"

"I can. The question is, can you?"

She'd clasped his jaw in her hand and held him still while she kissed him. "I can wait forever for you, Cal Morrison."

"I wish. If I had the money, I'd go over there and bring you home myself."

"More coffee?" Laura asked, breaking into his reverie.

He smiled. "Sure. Thanks."

He'd repeated her line over and over again in his head. "I can wait forever for you, Cal Morrison." Shame flooded him. He hadn't waited, had he? Had she waited? She wasn't married, though he'd heard through the grapevine she'd dated European guys. He guessed maybe she had waited. Waited until she found out he was married. Of course, he'd never promised to wait forever. And it was not like he'd intended to marry Jane. Stuff kind of happened, and then he had to do the right thing.

Here he was feeling guilty when, probably, she could care less. By now, he figured she'd had at least a dozen affairs with guys ten times as smart as Cal with a thousand times as much money. She sure didn't give him a warm greeting today, either. It was obvious she was through with him. Who could blame her? He'd been married. And if Jane had listened to Cal, she'd still be here, and he wouldn't be wondering about Giselle Davenport.

Nah. He had to be honest with himself. Even if Jane had lived, Cal would still be wondering about Giselle. Not that he'd do anything about it, then or now. But he'd wonder, always wonder what life would have been like if he'd waited or she'd stayed.

"Almost time to pick up Bobby," Laura said.

Cal checked his watch, wolfed down the rest of his food, and pushed to his feet. Nothing to be gained with the what-ifs in life. He had his hands full dealing with reality. Cal pushed through the door, climbed into his truck, and headed for Pine Grove Elementary.

Chapter Two

Giselle stood by the sink after filling up the kettle, when the doorbell rang.

"Come in!" she called, feeling the wall for the plug.

Julia Davenport joined her in the kitchen. "I have the baked goods," she said, placing a bag on the countertop.

"Great. I put the hot water on a minute ago. What kind of tea do you want?"

"Got any vanilla?"

"I do." Giselle headed for the cabinet. She lifted out a round cannister, opened it, and sniffed a few tea bags until she found the right ones.

"I found a place online that sells a talking microwave," Julia said, taking off her coat.

"I don't need a microwave."

"Why not? Everyone has one."

"I bet it's expensive."

"It is. At least five hundred bucks. But I'm sure it's worth it."

"People prepared food long before the microwave."

"Can I buy it for you for Christmas?"

Giselle turned away, sensing heat in her cheeks. She hated charity.

"It's okay, Julia. I'd much rather have some audiobooks."

"We can get those from the library. We could drive over there after the grocery store."

"Fine. I'm going to have to make some steady arrangement for driving."

"I bet there's a mom who would love to have a little part-time work one morning a week. Why don't you call the Pine Grove Elementary principal?"

"Great idea! I'll do it tomorrow."

"Now, let's get this house set up."

"I don't know if you're strong enough to move furniture," Giselle said.

"I'm a moose. That's what Bill always said. Let's give it a go."

Giselle plucked a notebook out of her purse. "I have the plans for where everything should go here." She handed the book to Julia.

Together, the women got the furniture where it belonged and dragged the boxes into the appropriate rooms. Then, they made the bed. Giselle sorted lingerie and socks for the bureau while Julia hung up dresses, jackets, and pants in the closet.

When Julia left for a dental appointment, Giselle lay down on the bed for a nap. Exhaustion took over, and the next thing she heard was the front door opening. Panic set in.

"Who's there?" she cried out in anguish.

"I'm so sorry. I should have knocked, but I didn't want to disturb you." Julia entered her niece's house, carrying a shopping bag.

Giselle gave her aunt a hug. "You're right on time for tea. I'll put the kettle on."

"You're so self-sufficient. It's amazing."

"I've had a few years to adjust."

"Can't I be impressed?"

"Life goes on, Julia. No matter what."

"True."

"Chamomile or Vanilla Chai?" Giselle asked, on her way to the kitchen.

"Vanilla, please. I brought you some Christmas decorations."

"I'm not going to have a tree. No point."

"Can we put these up in the window, then?" Julia asked.

"Sure. I don't want people to think I'm a Scrooge."

Giselle took down mugs and pulled the vanilla tea from the cannister.

Julia joined her niece. "Do you need help?"

"Say 'when,' will you?"

"Sure."

"I brought some of Laura Dailey's scones." She rummaged through the shopping bag.

"Are you going to do Santa's Thrift Shop?"

"Me? No. That was Mom's thing. Not mine." Giselle put a piece of the confection in her mouth.

"But you always helped out."

"When I had perfect vision. But now? No."

"I'll help. I'm sure we can find others."

"There's probably a ton of dust and mold growing in the back room. Ugh. I've been afraid to dig too deep in there."

Julia patted Giselle's arm. "The children look forward to it. And when I told people you were moving home, everyone asked me if you were going to do it."

"And what did you say?"

"Said I didn't know. Had to talk to you first."

"If everything was normal, well, maybe. But the way things are..."

"People will pitch in."

"I don't want that. I don't want help. I don't want pity. I just want to be left alone." Giselle pushed to her feet and stomped to the bay window.

Through the fuzziness, she made out a snowball fight happening across the street. Her heart squeezed. Of course, it would be Cal. She recalled the many times he'd rifled one at her bottom with amazing accuracy.

She sighed and turned away. No sense torturing herself. Cal had a new life, a child, and probably a girlfriend. Julia came up behind her, laying a hand on her shoulder.

"It's time for you to get a life."

STANDING AT THE WINDOW, staring at Giselle's house, Cal answered the phone. "Why didn't you tell me Giselle was moving across the street?"

"Because I didn't know," his mother, Betty, said.

"Like I believe that. You know everything going on in Pine Grove."

"I did know she'd moved back a while ago. She moved in with Julia Davenport in late June, I think."

"June?" he asked, his eyebrows shooting up. "When were you going to tell me?"

"Didn't think you'd want to know. You two are old news."

"Yeah, well, old is new now that she's across the street."

"Oh?" Betty said, her tone warming. "Really? You're seeing her again?"

"What? No! Not really even speaking to her."

"Too bad."

"You always liked her, didn't you?"

"What's not to like? She's a sweet, charming girl."

"Oh? Not so sweet and charming when she left me with an engagement ring in my pocket to move to Europe, was she?"

"You had an engagement ring?"

"I thought you knew, Ma."

"That makes it worse, doesn't it?"

"It was what it was. It's over. Has been for a long time now." He shifted his weight but didn't take his gaze from Giselle's property.

"I'm sorry, Cal. You were so happy with her."

"Ancient history. What's she doing back here? And why is she living across the street?"

"Why are you asking me? She's a stone's throw away. Why don't you ask her?"

"You'd love that, wouldn't you?"

"It's not about me, Son. It's about you. You have no life outside of Bobby. Why don't you go over there? Talk to her. Maybe you two can patch things up?"

"No way, Ma. No way." He shook his head.

"Not with a bad attitude."

"She's been gone a long time. I'm surprised she isn't married. It wouldn't be the same."

"You never know. It might be better."

"Yeah, right. I doubt she's interested in me, either. With all those European men. Besides, I've been married, have a son. Most women don't want men with kids."

"You never know until you try."

"You know everyone. Find out why she bought the house across the street. Okay?"

"I'll do my best."

"I gotta go," he said. "Love you." And hung up. Not that he had anything scheduled. It being a cold, windy day, there would be no tree work. He focused on Giselle's house again. He remembered the family who had lived there before her. They'd had one child, a girl, who'd played with Bobby. Then the woman got pregnant, so they moved.

Why would a woman without kids want to live so close to a school? The house needed repairs. From his window, he could see the front steps were uneven and chipped on the corners. He remembered there was a cracked window in the basement.

He hadn't seen a car. Did Giselle own a sleek European model, or did she buy American? He guessed she'd prefer European in cars, same as she did in men. The car must be in the garage. But there were no tire tracks in the snow. Maybe she was waiting for a delivery.

Questions about Giselle Davenport clouded his mind. He turned to face his living room. The carpet needed vacuuming, and Bobby had left toys strewn throughout. Damn, he'd have to teach that boy to pick up after himself. Cal was alone. He didn't have a woman to help with the chores.

After putting Bobby's toys in a pile, he called him into the room.

"Bring these back to your room, Bobby. You can't leave toys all over the house. It's okay to play with them in here, but then you have to take them back to your room. I need to vacuum and I can't do it with your stuff in the way."

"Sorry, Dad," the boy responded, picking up as many trucks as his little arms could carry.

Cal grinned and scooped up the rest.

"Why don't you play outside while I clean in here? See if Malcolm is around, or build a snowman, okay? I'll call you when dinner's ready."

He helped the boy on with his down jacket, mittens, and boots. Cal remained at the front door, watching his son run down the front path and across the street. Malcolm was building a snowman on his front lawn, and Bobby joined right in.

Cal sighed. It was sad Jane would miss watching her son grow up, gratitude for the child filled his heart. There was no greater gift than Bobby. Although Jane hadn't been the love of his life, he missed her sharing the parenting experience. His parents picked up the slack whenever they could. Bobby loved them and enjoyed being at their house where the rules weren't so strict.

Parenting alone sucked, but Cal had resigned himself to his fate. He smiled and closed the door, returning to his task.

FORTUNATELY, SHE DIDN'T need much at the grocery store. When Julia pulled to the curb, Giselle got out of the car and retrieved her bag from the backseat. After she bade her aunt goodbye, her ears zeroed in on the sound of little boy voices. She smiled.

She understood the lure of fresh snow to young boys, even on an icy day. Her coat wasn't thick enough, and the winterish wind penetrated, chilling her bones. She picked her way across the slippery walk, keeping her gaze trained on the sidewalk. Although her central vision was blurry, she still had reasonable peripheral vision. Turning her head, she spied the breaks in the ice and slowly made her way down her own front path.

Pow! Bam! Giselle flew to the left, landing on the hill on her front lawn. The snow softened the fall. The wind got knocked out of her, and her groceries scattered across the icy turf. As she struggled for breath, she heard crying.

"I'm sorry. I'm sorry. I didn't mean to hit you. I slipped," came tumbling out of the mouth of a little boy.

Giselle angled her head. Was it Cal's little boy, blubbering away?

Within a moment, she'd recovered her breath. Lying in the snow, she spoke.

"I'm okay. I know you didn't mean to hit me."

Then the crying stopped, and in its place, the rapid-fire of words.

"I'm sorry. Daddy's gonna be mad. Malcolm was chasing me, and I slipped and—"

"It's okay, Bobby," she said, holding up her hand.

"How do you know my name?"

"I know your father," she replied. "Do you think you could help me gather my groceries?"

"Sure." Bobby gathered the cans and boxes, and Giselle packed them in the bag. Sitting up, her bottom on the cold ground, she shivered.

Peering from the side, she noticed Bobby's lips were pale. "Are you cold?"

He nodded, hugging himself for a second. "Daddy said to stay outside while he vacuums."

"Would you like to come in for some hot chocolate?"

"Hot chocolate?"

"I have caramel hot chocolate."

"That's my favorite."

She figured he'd made it up, but she didn't care. "Okay. Let's go."

"I can't."

"Why not?"

"I'm not supposed to go into a house with a stranger."

"Oh. Of course. What if you ran home and asked your father? Tell him Giselle invited you?"

"Yeah. Gazelle?"

"No. Jizz-elle."

"Oh. Jizz-elle."

"Go ahead. Ask him." She tucked her knees underneath her and pushed up. "Bobby!" she cried as her feet skidded. He reached out, and she steadied herself by holding on to his shoulder with one hand and the bag with the other.

"Can you help me get inside?" she asked.

"Sure."

Together, they walked to her front door. She tried not to put her weight on his shoulder, but to use him only to keep her steady. When she arrived, she thanked him.

"You deserve a big mug of cocoa for helping. Ask Dad then come back and ring my bell."

"Okay," he said, and was off like a shot. She fumbled putting her key in the lock then opened the door. Thrusting the bag across the floor, she pushed it ahead then stepped into the foyer. She kept the house on the cool side, but it felt warm. She dumped her coat on a hook, grabbed the bag, and plopped it on the kitchen counter.

Gizelle turned on the radio to a station that played Christmas music 24/7. She sang along, keeping an ear tuned to the doorbell. Sure enough, it rang.

"I'm so glad you could come, Bobby. Come on in. We take our shoes off at the door in my house. Do you need help?"

Once his boots rested by the entryway, she led him to the kitchen.

"Do you like Christmas music?"

He nodded and took a seat.

As she gathered the ingredients for hot chocolate, she chatted with him about the holiday. The boy wasn't shy and went on about what he wanted Santa to bring him.

Giselle served the cocoa.

"Wow," Bobby said, after his first sip.

She opened a box from The Cozy Café. It had been filled with Christmas cookies. Though they had broken during the fall, she figured they'd still taste good. She put some on a plate.

"Jess Lennox made these." She put the plate in front of him, and he took one.

"Where's your husband?" Bobby asked with a mouthful of cookie.

Giselle sensed her cheeks color. "I don't have one."

"My dad doesn't have a wife, either."

"I see." *But I bet every available female for fifty miles is chasing him.*

"Do you have any kids?" the boy asked.

She shook her head. "Not even a dog. Just me."

"My dad has me. My mom died. I have a grandpa and grandma, too."

"Oh. I'm so sorry about your mom."

The boy nodded but kept chewing.

Peering at him from the side, she noticed his resemblance to his father was remarkable. Giselle's heart squeezed. She wanted to hug him, but he wasn't hers, and you simply didn't hug other people's kids, especially when you didn't know them well.

A few moments after he finished his chocolate, the doorbell rang.

"You shouldn't open your door without using the peephole," Cal said.

Giselle pressed her lips together into a fine line. No way would she tell him she couldn't see through the damn thing anyway.

"There's no one dangerous here." She raised her chin.

"You never know. I've come for Bobby. I don't want him to overstay his welcome."

"He hasn't. Come in."

"No, thanks. I'll wait here."

Giselle called to the boy, who came running. "Your dad's here. Let's get your boots on."

Not wanting to slam the door in Cal's face, no, wait, she did want to but held back. Leaving the door open would cool the house down. Damn him for not coming in. It was not like she'd proposed marriage to him. She'd simply asked him to step inside. Stubborn man. *Some things never change.*

"Daddy, Giselle doesn't have a husband. She doesn't have any kids, either. Maybe she'd like to be my mommy?" Bobby rambled on, embarrassing her until she couldn't face Cal.

"I don't think so, Bobby. She's happy right where she is."

"She's all by herself. She doesn't even have a dog," the boy remarked.

Nope. Too easy to trip over dogs.

Cal shifted his weight and shrugged.

"Thanks, Bobby. Maybe I can't be your mom, but I can be your friend. You can come over again for hot chocolate and cookies."

"I can?" the boy asked then turned to his father. "Can I, Dad?"

Cal scowled at her before opening his mouth. "I suppose. Yes. You can. As long as she invites you."

"I like her. She's nice," Bobby said.

Giselle hid a smile as she zipped up the boy's jacket.

"What do you say to Giselle, Bobby?" his father prompted.

"Thank you," he said then threw his arms around her and hugged her legs.

Bobby's simple gesture brought tears to the backs of her eyes as she held him close.

"I like you, too, Bobby. And you're welcome," she choked out, releasing the boy.

"Let's go." Cal put an arm around his son's shoulders and steered him outside.

She stood at the door, clutching the knob, watching them cross the street. They stopped for a car, and Bobby waved. She returned the gesture. *What a charming child.*

Damn. Cal had done a fine job raising the boy without a wife. She guessed he was self-sufficient. Except Bobby wanted a mother. With a rueful smile, she shut and locked the door. It wasn't her place to tell him that you don't always get what you want in life. She sighed and turned up the thermostat.

Chapter Three

"Leave your boots in the kitchen. I vacuumed the living room." After Cal removed his own shoes, he opened the pantry door and searched for a can of soup. Sure, he took as many cooking shortcuts as he could. He was a tree cutter, not a master chef. The doctor said Bobby was right on schedule with his growth and development, so Cal didn't worry.

He found a can of tomato soup.

"Grilled cheese and tomato soup," he said.

"Oh boy! Grilled cheese," Bobby responded.

Cal chuckled. It had been his favorite when he was a boy, too. After Jane died, his mother had taught him how to make it so he and Bobby could eat comfort food whenever they needed it.

He added milk to the soup then took out the cheese. His thoughts turned to Giselle. Damn, she'd been on his mind too much lately. He argued it wasn't his fault. It was not like he was horny or anything, or, even if he was, it was because she lived across the street. And he had to keep looking at her.

She still had the trim figure that turned him on as a teen. Hell, everything got him hard when he was sixteen. Today, he couldn't stop staring at her breasts. Were they a little fuller than he remembered? His fingertips recalled the softness of her skin. Her butt appeared a touch rounder than it had been six years ago.

And her mouth. Damn! With lipstick mostly worn off, her lips were a delicate pink, perfectly sweetheart shaped, and called to him. No, no, no! He had to stop this line of thinking. Okay, so maybe he still wanted to sleep with her. He was a man, after all, wasn't he? But it was only sex, hormones, whatever—nothing more!

Self-control would be his mantra. Not that she'd offered him anything. In fact, she'd been downright nasty. Probably for the best. He had to stay away from her, even if he couldn't shake the feeling, she still belonged to him. Especially, since it wasn't true.

When Bobby praised her, her cheeks had flushed. Damn, the woman was still beautiful! Cal couldn't deny it. If anything, her beauty had grown since she left Pine Grove. Standing at the door in her leggings with a flannel shirt barely covering her little butt, she personified a wet dream—his wet dream. He'd wanted to kiss her.

She probably would have slugged him. He needed to respect her boundaries. That's what she'd say. Oh, yes, Giselle now had the polish and sophistication of a European woman. Though he'd made fun of her sophistication to his parents, it only made him want her more.

Could she have been clearer about her feelings for him? Or lack thereof? Cold? Hell, he could freeze meat with the stare from her blue eyes. But she'd been nice to Bobby, warm with the boy. Sure, he needed a mother, but Giselle Davenport would never want the job.

Still, as he stood there with them, Cal couldn't help but think how different things would be if Bobby had been their child together. What would life be like now if she'd stayed home and they'd married and had a child? She'd still belong to him, and he'd be a much happier man.

It wasn't true. He wouldn't have Bobby. The boy had a good piece of his mother in him, like his friendliness and warmth. Jane had started the conversation with Cal in the bar where they'd met. She'd laughed, flirted, and joked with him. Bobby was her child.

Cal had always been quiet, thoughtful, and kept to himself, except around Giselle. She brought out his playful side. They'd romped in the snow, gone water-skiing on the lake, snow skiing on the mountain, hiking and bird-watching together. He'd teased her constantly in high school. It was his way of getting her attention. Damn, he'd loved those days.

Now, his life was solitary. He didn't mind much, made it easier to get things done. But for one instant, standing at her door, Bobby hugging her legs, he'd allowed his mind to imagine Bobby was their child. And it had blown him away.

The phone rang.

"Got a couple of plow jobs, Cal. You free?" his father asked.

"Sure. I'll take Bobby with me."

"Okay. Be careful. Mrs. Ghent, the Robinson's, and Bill Tolliver. Got that?"

"Yep. I'll head out as soon as we finish dinner."

"Where we goin', Dad?" Bobby asked, between sips of soup.

"Wanna ride in the plow with me?"

"In the plow?"

"Yep. We've got some driveways that need doin'."

"Yes!" The boy bolted up from the table.

Cal raised his hand. "Whoa. Wait a minute. Finish your dinner first."

"Do I have to?"

"Yes, you do. Me, too."

Cal watched Bobby eat. Proud of the fact he could cook enough for them to live and make enough money to afford a small house, Cal patted himself on the back from time to time. Making lemonade out of lemons wasn't easy, but when he was done, he was satisfied.

When they finished, Cal layered warm clothing on himself and his son before heading outside. He glanced up and noticed Giselle's driveway hadn't been plowed. Maybe that was why she hadn't taken her car out of the garage? He'd seen her get in and out of Julia's car. But she had to brave the front steps, which weren't safe, rather than come out from the side door right to the driveway.

The blacktop sported a foot of untouched snow. Maybe they could clear it on their way home. Damn, there he went again, thinking about her. Why did she have to move across the street? And would he forever be wanting something he couldn't have?

ALTHOUGH, GISELLE HAD set up the basics in the house, the next morning, there was much more to do. Packed boxes ended up in the spare bedroom. She dreaded the task of finding perfect spots for her possessions.

With a heavy heart, she admitted moving her huge collection of books had been a stupid idea. She could read, but only at great effort, using a special light and magnifier. Audio books had replaced written reading material. Making her way to what had now become the storage room, she stopped in the doorway and sighed. The doorbell sounded.

Grinning at the reprieve from the onerous task, she greeted her visitor.

"Aunt Julia! What a delightful surprise."

"Get your coat, young lady. We're going out to breakfast." Julia stood, legs spread, hands on hips on the front step, letting cold air in the house.

"Great! Give me a sec." Giselle went to her bedroom where she rummaged around in her closet for her warmest coat. After putting it on, she returned to her aunt, and, arm in arm, the two women picked their way along the icy path to Julia's car.

"Where to?" Giselle asked.

"The Cozy Café. Best breakfast in Pine Grove." Julia turned onto Main Street.

"This tiny town? That's not saying much."

Julia laughed.

Once they were seated, Amy, the owner, brought menus.

"Coffee, ladies?" she asked.

They nodded, and Amy filled two mugs already on the table. "Whatcha having this morning?"

They ordered bacon, eggs, and cinnamon buns. Then Julia spoke. "Well, look at that."

"What?"

"I guess you can't make it out. There's a small poster on the bulletin board."

"What's it say?" Giselle looked down, focusing on adding milk to her coffee.

Julia read, "Volunteers wanted. Giselle Davenport is back and needs help to open Santa's Thrift Shop. Interested? Call Julia Davenport."

Giselle's head shot up. "You?"

"I didn't put it there. I don't know why they listed my name and number," Julia said, raising her palms.

"Maybe because you gave it to them?" Giselle cocked an eyebrow at her aunt.

"No, I didn't. Honest. Maybe they didn't know yours."

"I told you, I'm not doing it."

"And if we get volunteers?"

"Then I'll have to tell them. About me. And the sight thing."

"So? Won't everyone find out eventually anyway?" Julia asked.

"They won't if I don't talk about it."

Amy brought cinnamon buns.

"Oh yeah. I get it." Julia nodded her head.

"Get what?"

"You mean Cal Morrison will find out, don't you?"

Giselle couldn't keep the heat from her cheeks. Julia had hit it right on the head.

"He's living across the street from you. Is he a moron? No. Then he'll figure out something isn't kosher sooner or later." Julia took a bite of her pastry.

"Can I opt for later?"

"You're being silly. He's so close by. What if you need help? He's right there."

"I don't need anything from him." Giselle sniffed, raising her chin slightly.

"Yes, you do. Or you will. You might. Hasn't growing up in Pine Grove taught you anything?"

"What do you mean?"

"I mean we all need each other. That's what small town living is all about. Maybe if you lived in a gigantic apartment building in New York City, you could get away with it. But not here. Eventually, you'll need something. And Cal is there."

"Can't I need something from someone else?"

Julia laughed. "Just as stubborn as your father. We Davenports are a determined lot. Life will be a lot easier...*nicer* for you, if you face the disability and tell the truth."

"So you say. I disagree."

"Look at that poster. And I swear, I didn't put it up. People want Santa's Thrift Shop. And they're willing to help."

"We'll see how many volunteers we get."

Julia smiled. "Good. You're open to the idea."

"Maybe."

"What we need is a carpool. If you could get rides to and from the shop, you could handle things there."

"Don't be so sure people will flock to volunteer." Giselle cut off a piece of the bun and put it in her mouth.

"Don't be so sure they won't," Julia replied.

The women finished their breakfast and started for Giselle's place. On the way, Julia got three calls. Once in the living room, Giselle lit a fire in the fireplace while Julia manned her phone.

Settling into the sofa, Giselle bemoaned her burden of unpacking and placing her books.

"Books? Too many books?" Julia asked.

Giselle nodded.

"Why not donate them to the thrift shop? They'd make great Christmas gifts for the kids to give their parents, aunts, and uncles."

"What a brilliant idea!" Giselle bounced up from the sofa and paced. "Let's see how many boxes I have."

Together, the women counted fifteen boxes of books.

Giselle reached down to lift one. "They're heavy."

"I've got it! One of the calls was Jess Lennox West. She said they don't use the car all day and the chauffeur could ferry you back and forth to the thrift shop every day. He's a strong guy. He can schlep these boxes over there for you."

"Perfect!" A smile broke out on Giselle's face. "That's a great solution."

"Good. And now you have to open Santa's Thrift Shop," Julia pointed out.

"Did you get any other volunteers?"

"Two more people, and I have a dozen texts here, too. People as far away as Oak Bend. Geez, where the hell did Laura place those posters?" Julia rubbed her chin.

"Laura? Laura Dailey?"

It was her aunt's turn to blush.

"I thought you didn't know who put up that poster?" Giselle asked.

"Okay. It was my idea. Laura loved it and volunteered. She sent Barney out with them early this morning."

"I thought so. She knew your phone number instead of mine. Bunch of baloney."

Julia grabbed her niece's arm. "Look. You're trapped in here all day long. All by yourself. You need to get out. Be with people. This isn't healthy. And you need help. Don't turn your back on this. It'll be good for you and the community."

Giselle hugged her. "You're right. I guess it's time for me to face the music."

"Time for you to get some support from your hometown."

Giselle sank onto the sofa. "Okay. Just not Cal. All right?"

"Suit yourself. But I think you're making a mistake."

CAL STOPPED BY THE Cozy Café for breakfast. He spied the poster on the wall.

"Santa's Thrift Shop?" Cal directed the question to Laura, who took his order. "Is that back in business?"

"Yep. Looks like Giselle's doin' Santa's Thrift Shop," Laura Dailey said. "Pickin' up where her mother left off."

"Hmm," Cal muttered into his coffee.

"Seems they need volunteers. You fixin' to help?" She cast a sidelong glance at him.

"Me? Nah. I've got stuff to do. Taking care of Bobby. Plowing. I'm on emergency call."

"Oh yeah. So far, though, no bad weather. I'm sure she could use a big, strong guy like you over there."

"Don't worry about Giselle. She'll manage to get any help she needs."

He finished and headed for the parking lot. Curiosity grabbed him. Though snow fell, Cal drove by the thrift shop instead of going straight home. Looked like word had gotten out. There were boxes piled high against the building's small front porch. Bags of donations filled any empty spaces. If the snow continued, the items in the bags might get ruined. Cal pulled into the parking lot and ambled over to the side door. When he located the key under the mat, he grinned. Mrs. Davenport always hid the key there. He chuckled to think the whole town probably knew.

After unlocking the door, he went in and looked around. A large empty space by a window appeared to be big enough. Cal toted the boxes in one by one and stacked them neatly by the wall. Then he arranged the bags in front of the cartons.

When he finished, he locked the door and drove home. Sure, Giselle could handle those boxes, but why shouldn't he help? No one had to know. Cal contributed to all the events in Pine Grove, including donations to the thrift shop. If he didn't have anything gently used, he went out and bought a few items.

He'd hung out there a few times with Giselle in high school. They'd pitched in with her mother to get the unique shop off the ground. They'd helped kids select gifts for their families, and even wrapped them for younger children.

Memories of fun times, drinking Lucy Davenport's famous hot chocolate, and eating cookies donated by Laura Dailey as they worked, warmed him. At the end of the day, they'd locked up and Cal would drive Giselle home, but not before stealing a few kisses behind the store.

The innocence and sweetness of those times squeezed his heart. These days, the challenges of his life prevented him from indulging in those pursuits. He bounced from one responsibility to another then flopped into bed, tired and alone. Those had been wonderful times. He counted himself lucky to have known such fine people and to receive kisses from the prettiest girl in school.

Once he arrived home, Cal set about preparing stew for dinner. He only needed a glance out the kitchen window to see a storm brewing. Clouds darkened from light gray to a more ominous color. Snow still trickled down with tiny flakes melting on his window.

Once the ingredients were in the pot, he shrugged a jacket over his shoulders and headed for the wood pile. He stuffed two bundles of logs under his arms and returned inside. They needed enough for two days of fires, if the radio had been correct. Already, the snowfall had increased. He shook the icy water off his head before entering the house.

After placing the logs by the fireplace, he checked the cabinets. The stash of marshmallows looked low. He made a mental note to buy more next shopping trip. Without a woman to tell them "no," Bobby and Cal roasted marshmallows every time they lit a fire.

Should Bobby have so much sugar? Probably not, but Cal didn't care. The boy didn't have a mother, there had to be some compensations. Cal chose marshmallows, along with rides on the snowplow, and other activities that would make a mother blanch, to make the boy's life special. Other kids had moms, but they didn't get to ride around town on a snowplow in the dead of winter.

Cal stopped at the front window to check out Giselle's place. She inched her way down the slippery walk toward her mailbox. He shook his head. *Where the hell are her boots?* He wanted to turn away but couldn't. Finally, he threw open the door and strode across the street. Opening her postbox, he snatched the mail inside and then joined her.

"Here. Where are your boots?"

"I didn't realize it was this slippery."

"Didn't you look?" he asked, anger tinging his tone.

"I-I-I didn't see the ice."

"Well, it's there. Next time, look. Or just put on boots. This is Pine Grove, remember? You grew up here. I wear out a pair of boots every year. You're going to get hurt if you don't dress for the weather."

"Thank you." She took the mail from his hand, ignoring his admonishment.

"Suit yourself. But when you fall and break something, don't cry for me."

She stiffened. "Don't worry, Cal, I won't. I could be dying on the ground and I wouldn't call for you," she said, her tone colder than a glacier.

He stepped back, as if he'd been slapped. "Pardon me for trying to help."

"Is that what you were trying to do? Help? Seemed more like seizing an opportunity to yell at me. What's eating you, Cal? It's been a million years. You got over me in thirty seconds. You married someone else. What gives you the right to be so hostile to me?"

"Got over you in thirty seconds? I'm not the one who walked out, who took off for Europe. I'm not the one who left me high and dry. Who agreed, in five seconds, to date other people? That wasn't me, lady. You practically told me to find someone else. I can't help it if you didn't."

Her jaw tightened, and her lips compressed into a thin line. "Whether I found someone else or not is none of your business."

"Damn right it isn't. And my marriage isn't any of yours."

"Leave me alone, Cal." Straightening her shoulders, she pushed by him.

"My pleasure," he said, making an exaggerated bow to her back.

She stopped and called over her shoulder. "And it was you who said we should see other people. Don't hang that on me." She tossed her hair and continued on her way.

Gripping the handrail, Giselle went up her steps slowly but without incident. Cal stood, watching. There was something about her, something different. He couldn't put his finger on it, but Giselle had never been wobbly before. Of course, it had been six years, but she was still young. What had happened to make her so unsure on the path and the steps?

She must be hiding whatever it was. Just like Giselle, never wanting to admit she was less than perfect. Well, hell, she'd sure told him off. Why should he even be curious? She'd ordered him to leave her alone, and that's exactly what he'd do.

Cal brushed the snow off his sleeves and trudged home. Giselle Davenport made it completely clear she wasn't his concern. Didn't he have enough to worry about without adding her to the list? He'd take her advice and bug off. Time to face the fact she didn't belong to him anymore, and probably never had.

Stopping to stir the stew, he checked his watch. Almost time to pick up Bobby. Cal grinned. Bobby bounded into his life, his home, with energy and enthusiasm. No one could stay depressed with that little ball of fire around. With a quick glance at the DVD shelf, he spied the perfect movie to enjoy with his son. *Homeward Bound* was their favorite. Neither man nor child tired of that film. He zipped up his heaviest jacket and set out for the walk to school, grateful to have his son...and suddenly sorry for Giselle to have nothing and no one.

THE KNOCK ON THE DOOR startled Giselle. Busy arranging wood in the fireplace, she hadn't expected anyone.

"Who is it?"

"Chris Toller. Jess West sent me? Did anyone tell you?"

She opened the door. "Please, come in. It's freezing out there."

The man stomped the snow off his feet before he stepped inside. Giselle stared hard at him then angled her head to get a better view from the side. He appeared to be around her age and nice looking, with brown hair.

"I'm supposed to drive you to the thrift store and pick you up to go home."

"Oh! Yes, my aunt, Julia, said something about it. I'm not planning to go there today. I have some excellent hot chocolate on the stove, won't you have some with me?"

"That's mighty kind. Sounds good on a day like today."

"What's the temperature outside?" she asked, leading him to the kitchen.

"Last time I checked, it was eighteen. Supposed to drop to zero tonight."

"Is it snowing?" she asked.

"Yes, ma'am."

"Please, call me Giselle." She put her hand on his forearm.

"Can I help? What can I do?"

"You can pour. I'll get the mugs." Bustling around from one cabinet to the next, she found two mugs, napkins, and spoons. After she stirred the small pot on the stove, Chris picked it up and filled the cups.

They sat at the table.

"So, you're not planning to go over there today?"

"No. It's a bit slick outside. But I do have something you can do."

"Anything."

"I have quite a few boxes of books that need to go over there."

"I can do that."

"Good. I'll show you where they are."

Chris took a sip. "Wow, you were right. This hot chocolate is amazing."

"It's hazelnut hot chocolate. A special blend my mother made."

Giselle put the dishes in the sink then led Chris to the spare room. Then she held the door open as he hauled box after box out to the car. A twinge shot through her as she watched her beloved books, like old friends, leave the house. She took a deep breath. Not knowing which books were gone might be easier than poring through them under a bright light and a magnifier and deciding about each one. She'd been passionate about reading and research. But why keep books she couldn't use? No reason.

When Chris had half the boxes loaded, he declared the car full. "I'll take these over and stack them up in the shop. Is it unlocked?"

"No, but there's a key under the mat by the side door."

"Great. I'll drive them over now. Do you plan to go tomorrow?"

She hugged herself and sighed. "Guess I'd better."

"Is it okay if I come around at nine?"

"Perfect. Thank you so much, Chris."

"No problem. And thanks for the hot chocolate."

She stood at the door and watched him drive off. Something moved across the street. She figured it must be Cal. *Watching me? Good. Let him wonder what Chris is doing here.* Stepping back inside, Giselle closed the door. The house had cooled off, and she shivered.

After making her way to the fireplace, Giselle lit the logs then retrieved a sweater from her room. She curled up on the love seat, wrapping a throw around her legs. The crackling of the burning wood soothed her. Cold had seeped into her bones and her heart.

When had living alone become so hard? Having Cal across the street, examining her every move only made life more stressful. How much longer could she keep her secret from him? And if he found out? Ugh. She shuddered. He'd think she was some cripple, some subnormal human being. Surely, she wouldn't be worth his time.

Hadn't Gunther, her German fiancé, made it perfectly clear he'd never marry a woman who wasn't physically perfect. Nope, not for him. He admitted that caretaking wasn't in his wheelhouse. In the end, she'd realized losing him had been no loss at all. A shallow, selfish man, he'd taken up too much of her time. Had she loved him? No way. He'd never measure up to Cal Morrison, the man she used to judge every other man under the sun. But she'd been lonely, in Europe away from her family, and Gunther had wanted her.

Perhaps getting immersed in Santa's Thrift Shop would assuage her loneliness, at least for a little while. She smiled as happy memories of days there with her mother returned. She closed her eyes and, for a moment, could feel her first kiss, behind the store, from Cal. She drifted off to sleep, snuggled under the blanket and heated by the fire.

Chapter Four

After returning from dropping Bobby at school, Cal tramped through the snow on his front lawn to the front porch. As he toed off his boots, he noticed a car pull up to Giselle's house. A good-looking man around Cal's age got out and rang her bell. She opened the door and he went in.

Cal entered his house and headed for the kitchen. He washed his hands then threw the fixings for chicken soup into his Crock-Pot and turned it on. When he got back to the window, the vehicle was still parked there.

A wave of jealousy washed over him, practically knocking him down. He pictured various scenarios that made him sick to his stomach. *What is that guy doing there? Who is he? Why's he there so long? How does she know him? Is she dating him? Is she sleeping with him?* He had a ton of questions, but no answers.

He sank down on the sofa but kept his gaze on the street in front of her house. Why should he give a damn? Maybe that guy's dating her, so what? What's it to Cal? He didn't want to go out with her, right? The more he tried to talk himself out of caring, the more his stomach clenched. He bent over, burying his face in his hands.

The truth shot through him like an electrical shock. He did still care for Giselle, maybe more than ever. He worried about her living alone. It was why he'd chopped firewood for her and added it to her woodpile, why he'd hauled the boxes inside the thrift shop, plowed her driveway, why he kept his eye on her 24/7. Misery swept him. Damn. He still loved her. And she hated him. What the hell?

What could this guy do for her that Cal couldn't? Could he plow her driveway? Cal doubted it. But he could. And he'd shovel the walk, split wood, make chicken soup when she was sick, mow her lawn. Make love to her. There wasn't anything this guy could do better than Cal.

Finally, the man left the house and drove away. He watched Giselle stand in the doorway, waving at him. She didn't wave at Cal. She'd told him to leave her alone. To be fair, he'd yelled at her, but still. He didn't want to leave her alone. He wanted to be with her, every day. He wanted Bobby to love her. But most of all, and he took a deep breath at this revelation, he wanted her to belong to him and to love him again like she did years ago. But it was too late for that, wasn't it?

A deep rumble interrupted his pity party. He glanced up at the sky. The clouds darkened and roiled around, threatening. With wind whipping snow against his face, Cal hit the woodpile again, stuffing a load under each arm. Inside, he switched on the radio to the local station, listening for a weather report, as he brushed snow off his jacket.

He called his folks.

"Looks like a big storm about to hit, Ma."

"I think so. You stocked up?"

"Yep. I stopped at the store yesterday. Can you take Bobby if I get called on an emergency?"

"I sure can."

"Say, Ma, heard anything about Giselle?"

"Like what?" his mother asked, her tone guarded.

"I don't know. Like maybe she's dating someone?"

"Dating someone? Who?"

"That's what I'm asking you."

Betty Morrison laughed. "You're living across the street from her. Did you see anyone come a-calling?"

"I saw a car this morning. Pretty fancy. Shiny black. One of those expensive kinds."

"You mean Stryker West's Bentley?"

"Black?" Cal asked.

"Yep."

"Could be. He's not running around on his wife already, is he?"

"I doubt it. But it could be his chauffeur, Chris," Betty replied.

"Oh. Okay. So, he's dating Giselle?"

"Not that I've heard."

"Hmm. Maybe it hasn't gotten around to you yet."

"I doubt that. Everything gets to my door pretty quick. He and Stryker used to go to the Cozy for breakfast every morning. Now that he's married, I doubt Stryker does, but Chris might. Maybe you can meet up with him there and ask him yourself."

"No, no. I mean it's none of my business." Cal took a breath.

"Then why are you askin'? And why don't you make it your business? What are you waiting for, Cal, the next millennium? Ask the woman out. You know you want to. We'll take Bobby if you're going out."

"Who says I want to ask her out?" Cal's voice raised an octave.

"I do. That's who."

"Ma, don't butt in."

"Someone either needs to hit you in the head with a hammer or a cattle prod. Boy, you know you still care for her. Get off your butt before someone else does."

"Ma, don't interfere."

"I'm just pointing out to you what everyone else in the entire world can see."

"No, they can't."

"Oh, yes, they can. And they tell me daily. Someone even saw you putting boxes in the thrift shop to get them out of the snow."

"So? I helped at the thrift shop. Big fuckin' deal."

"Cal?"

"Sorry."

"People see what you, obviously, can't. It must be drivin' you nuts to live across the street from her and keep your distance."

Cal lowered his head. As usual, his mother had hit it on the head.

"Okay. I admit it. Bobby's already made friends with her. He stops there almost every day to mooch a free hot chocolate."

"See?"

"Too much time has passed. Too much went on or didn't."

"Why don't you pick up where you left off?"

"I wish I could, Ma. I wish I could."

His mother snorted into the phone. "That's a crock. You haven't even tried, have you? Approached her nice or anything."

"No."

"But I'm bettin' you've yelled at her?"

"You got a sixth sense, Ma."

"Yelling isn't going to get you anywhere with her. And next time, she might slug you. I sure as heck would."

"She's not dating anyone?" Cal asked.

"Not that I've heard. But she will be before long if you don't get over there first. I gotta go. It's so damn frustrating to talk to you. Stubborn as a mule. Worse than your father. Bring Bobby over whenever you need to. I'll be home."

Cal put his phone on the counter. Maybe his mother was right. He peered out the window. Snow, heavy and blowing sideways, obstructed his view. Smoke curled up from Giselle's chimney. Should he go over there? Did he have a good reason? No, but it never stopped him before.

Like a complete idiot, he dressed in boots and shrugged on his jacket and grabbed a snow shovel. No one shovels while the wind is blowing, and the snow was still coming down. But hell, shoveling her walk was his only excuse to go over there.

He opened the door and cursed the snow that blew into his kitchen. It didn't take long for the icy precipitation to sting his face as he tromped over to her place. He started in on the steps. Thank

God the walkway was short because he'd begun to lose sensation in his face. When he reached her doorway, he stopped. Like magic the door opened, and an angel stood there in leggings and a flannel shirt, holding a mug of hot chocolate.

THE SOUND OF SOMETHING scraping drew Giselle's attention. Sitting in front of the fire, sipping hot chocolate and listening to an audiobook, she found the sound annoying. It disrupted her attention. Turning off the book, she went to the window, hoping to make out where it was coming from.

The blizzard outside obscured everything. But the whiteness of the snow brightened the image. She could make out the figure of a person on her walkway. From the movement, she guessed someone was shoveling snow.

Giselle smiled. Country people lending a helping hand to those who needed it—something she'd always loved about Pine Grove folks. But who could it be? Couldn't be Cal. He wouldn't be caught dead over here, helping her. Chris had gone home. She pressed her nose against the glass, hoping to get a better look.

Her peripheral vision picked up a deep peacock blue on the torso. Damn! It was Cal! He'd worn the same colored jacket when she had her confrontation with him. Confused, she didn't know whether to smile at his thoughtfulness, or cringe at his lecture about how she needed to keep her walkway clear.

Opting for the positive assumption, she padded to the kitchen to warm up some chocolate for him. She knew her kitchen well, and it didn't take long to add a bit of hazelnut cream to the mixture and turn on the heat.

She watched the snow, pelting down in a fury outside, and shivered to think of him braving the furies of Mother Nature to help her. So, there was a shred of the old Cal she had known and fallen in love with.

When the beverage had heated through, she stopped at the front door. From what she could see, he was practically done. She opened the door, holding the mug in one hand.

"Come in. Warm up," she said, extending the drink.

He hesitated.

"It's okay. You can leave your boots by the door."

Suddenly, his large frame filled the space. She backed up. He toed off his boots, unzipped his jacket, removed his cap, and shook them off outside before taking the mug with two hands. Giselle took his coat and hung it on a peg.

"Come in. I have a fire going. It's wicked out there."

"You're telling me." He shook his head then followed her, put his mug on the coffee table, and knelt in front of the flames, holding his hands close to the heat. Giselle tucked her legs underneath her on the love seat.

"Thank you for shoveling my walk."

"No problem. Just being neighborly." He took a sip. "This is amazing. What's in it?"

"It's a secret."

"Bobby talks about it all the time. Now I know why. Tell me."

"If I do, then you'll make it for him, and he'll stop coming to see me."

She felt his stare. "Would that be so bad? I'm sure he's a pest."

"Bobby? No way. I love his company. He's fun."

"I think so. But he's my kid."

"You've raised him right. He's bright and sweet. We're listening to a Hardy Boys book."

"Listening?"

Giselle felt the blush in her face. She hadn't meant to give that away.

"I like to listen to books. I can do it while I'm doing something else. We're on chapter four."

"Hmm. He never said. Chapter four, eh?"

"Yes, he stops by when you let him out to play. We do one chapter and a mug of chocolate each visit."

Silence followed then the sound of him sipping. She didn't know if he was happy or angry.

"If you don't want him here, I understand."

"I didn't say that."

"Were you thinking it?"

"Never mind what I was thinking," he said, his tone gruff.

"So, do you mind or don't you?" she asked, trying not to sound impatient.

"Of course I don't mind. Bobby has a real crush on you. It does him good to be with you. Sometimes, I'm short with him. It's hard. I'm not as understanding about stuff as I should be."

"It must be hard to raise him alone," she said, instinctively reaching for his hand.

She touched the back and he turned it, folding his calloused fingers around her small ones. His touch startled her, and her breath caught in her throat. Memories of holding hands with Cal flooded back, warming her from the inside out.

There had always been something so special about holding hands. His were rough from the work he did, handling machines and equipment. Strong hands engulfed her small one, surrounding and protecting it. It had been the first thing about him that had made her heart skip a beat—holding hands.

After a few moments, he withdrew his. She smiled to cover the twinge of pain caused by the loss. Oh, how she'd wished for the strength of his hands, the warmth of his embrace when she'd gotten the news about her eyesight.

Gunther had been there when she'd returned from the doctor's office. Devastated and still trying to absorb the meaning of early onset macular degeneration, she'd stumbled toward him. After a quick hug, he'd held her at arm's length.

Seared into her brain were his hurtful words, "Don't expect me to become your nursemaid, Giselle. Don't expect me to wait on you or take care of you. You'll have to figure out how to deal with this on your own."

It had been only a week later he'd informed her they were over, and he'd found someone else. Cal Morrison would never have walked out on her. If they had been together, he'd have reassured her he still loved her. But at the time, he hadn't, didn't, wouldn't—he was married to someone else. The memory of the acute pain of that moment returned.

"So, it's okay if Bobby keeps coming here?" she asked.

"Yeah. Thank you. I appreciate what you're doing for him."

"Of course, when you get married again, he won't be coming here anymore. I understand."

Cal laughed. "Don't worry about that. Doesn't look like that's gonna happen, ever."

"Really?"

Silence.

"I...I, well. You know how I... I mean. Oh hell. I can't talk today." Cal rose to his feet. "I should be going."

"Have you warmed up?"

"Yes, more than necessary." He chuckled.

She laughed, embarrassed and happy at the same time.

"I've never seen a woman look so good in a flannel shirt," he blurted out.

"Thank you."

Giselle walked him to the door. With her mind occupied by thoughts of Cal, she didn't pay attention and tripped over his boots. He caught her. For a glorious moment, she rested in his arms, her cheek against the soft wool of his sweater. Cal's scent brought back happy memories. He closed his arms around her, and they stood together for an instant before he let go.

"Sorry," he said.

"Thank you for breaking my fall."

"Pleasure was all mine."

He put his coat, hat, and boots on, and cupped her cheek. She took his wrist and slid his palm to her lips. He bent down and brushed his over hers. Only for a second, a thrill shot through her. Then he was gone. A gust of wind blew snow into her entryway, swirling it around her. Giselle touched her lower lip, ignoring the icy drops. She hesitated then shut the door.

CAL BENT HIS HEAD AGAINST the wind and freezing flakes fluttering in his face. He'd kissed her. He'd kissed Giselle. And held her. God, it felt good to have her in his arms again. She smelled of hazelnut, chocolate, and expensive perfume. Her body, the same size as in high school, melted against his, reminding him of one of the many things he adored about Giselle Davenport—her softness.

Inside his house, he hung his wet gear in the bathroom then put up a pot of coffee. A glance at the clock told him Bobby would be getting out of school in half an hour. Enough time for his jacket to dry only to get soaked and cold one more time. His phone rang.

"Ike, here. Checking in with you, Cal. We're putting people on alert. Storm's due to get bad either tonight or tomorrow."

"I'm here. I made plans for my parents to take Bobby, so I'm available."

"Good. Let's hope the damn thing passes over us without much damage."

"Agreed."

"Talk to you later," Ike said.

Cal pulled on his boots and headed back into the frigid, icy wind. On the way home from school, Bobby jumped into the snow.

"Oh boy! Can I play outside, Dad?"

"Let's have a snack first then we'll see."

"But it's snowing."

"And it will still be snowing after we eat."

"Can I go to Giselle's?"

"After—yes."

Bobby kicked a small pile of snow then ran ahead, slowing down only where the snow got deep. When they reached home, Cal ladled chicken soup into bowls, and the guys chowed down. Bobby finished fast.

"There's a storm coming. If it gets bad, I'll have to go." Cal loaded the bowls into the dishwasher.

"Can't I come?"

Cal smiled. His son had all the right instincts. "Maybe when you're older."

"Aw, gee. I'm too young for anything," Bobby complained.

"Not too young for school. Your day will come. Go see if your friends can play outside. I'll be keeping my eye on you from the living room."

"Okay. And if they can't, can I go to Giselle's? We're on chapter four."

"Okay."

Cal helped his son on with his snow gear, and the boy ran out into the powdery wonderland. Cal brought a cup of coffee to the living room and opened the newspaper. When he glanced up, he could see his son tramping through the drifts from house to house. Some of those kids were kept inside by parents because of the freezing temperature and wind. Bobby was hardy. He loved the snow. The cold didn't seem to bother the boy.

He ended up at Giselle's, where he went inside. Cal didn't buy her story about audiobooks. He knew something was up but didn't have a clue as to what. And his mother knew it, too. He could tell by her cagey responses to his questions. He'd pry it out of her as soon as the storm was over. He hated being the last one to know a secret.

After about an hour or so, Bobby bounced home.

"I've got *Dunstan Checks In* ready. Let's make popcorn," Cal said, helping his son off with his wet gear.

Cal put the snack in a big bowl while Bobby turned on the television. Then the two curled up together on the sofa. Something about this movie, where the mom had died, seemed to soothe the boy. They watched it often, laughing together at the funny parts.

Now that Giselle was back, Cal wondered what it might have been like if they had married and had a child, like Bobby. Curling up with her and their offspring on a big sofa, eating popcorn, watching a movie together would have been sheer heaven. He sighed. No use dreaming about something that would never be. That time had passed. He ruffled Bobby's hair, grateful to have his son.

"If I get called out tonight, I'll take you to Grandma and Grandpa's house. Okay?"

"Okay. Do you think there'll be any emergencies?"

"With the way the wind is blowing, I'm betting there'll be trees down and power out."

"Then you go and save everybody?"

Cal laughed. "No, Son. I don't save people. I cut up the trees and get them off the road or off power lines. I plow. I do the cleanup."

"But doesn't that save people?"

"I suppose. Maybe in a roundabout sort of way. Helping to keep the power on, or clearing the way for the guys to fix the lines. And for fire engines and ambulances to get through."

"See?" Bobby said.

Cal chuckled at the look of triumph on the little boy's face.

While Cal started dinner, Bobby went to his room to build with blocks. The large kitchen window provided a view of the gathering storm. The tap-tap-tap of ice on the glass drew his eye. Trees bent in the wind, their branches doing a wild dance. Lights flickered.

Bobby raced into the room.

"Dad! My lights went out."

By the time Cal checked the house, Bobby's had come back on.

"I'm scared."

Cal knelt down to make eye contact. "No reason to be scared. You're safe, as long as you stay inside. No matter what happens, don't go outside, okay?"

The boy nodded then fell into his father's arms. The timer went off, and Cal stood up.

"Dinner."

They sat down to eat. As Cal finished his last bite of mac and cheese, the phone rang.

"Hey, Cal. Sorry to bother you, but we've got a couple of trees down, blocking Cedar Lake Drive and Elm Street."

"I'll pack up my son and drop him at my parents' place. Then, I'll be on my way."

"Emergency?" Bobby asked.

"Yep." Cal dialed his parents. "I'm bringing Bobby. Okay?"

"We're ready," his father said.

Cal donned his bad-weather gear, packed a few things for his son, and waited for Bobby to pick out a few toys. A scratchy message came across the radio. A pine tree toppled across Grace Church Street, stopping traffic.

Panic flowed through Cal. He picked up the phone.

"Dave, I can't leave. My parents are on Grace Church. I can't get there to drop off my son."

"We can't clear the pine off Grace Church yet. The damn tree took down an electrical wire, and it's live. Too dangerous. We have to wait until Con Ed gets there to shut off the power. Can you find someone else to fill in?"

Cal's phone beeped. "I've got an incoming call, I get back to you." He picked up the other call. It was his mother.

"I'm so sorry, dear. Our street is blocked. And they said they don't know when the wires will be fixed so the tree can be removed."

"I know, Ma. Dave at dispatch called."

"What are you going to do?"

"I don't know."

"I could call Giselle to come stay with Bobby. She's only across the street," Betty said.

"Giselle?"

"Yeah. You remember her." Betty chuckled.

"I don't have her number."

"Do you want me to call?"

"Give me the number. I'm not a baby. I'll call her."

"I don't see what other option you have."

"Right. Just hope she steps up to the plate."

"Me, too. Uh, if she doesn't, there might be a reason…"

"I don't have time for gossip. What's the number?"

After he punched it in his phone, he dialed.

"Giselle?"

"Yes?"

"It's Cal."

"Oh. Of course. How are you?"

"I'm fine. But I've got a situation with Bobby."

Cal explained the problem.

"Could you come here? It's blowin' like crazy. Thirty-mile-an-hour winds. Snow and ice comin' down."

"You want me to come to your house?"

"If you can. If that's all right."

"Of course I can. Of course it's all right. Okay. I'll be dressed and out of here in a few minutes."

"Thanks."

The phone clicked off. He took a big breath. Had no idea she'd agree. Maybe because it was for Bobby. She seemed to be fond of him. He certainly liked her. Cal let out a breath. Problem solved.

Cal called Dave back.

"Okay, Dave. I've got Bobby covered. Where do you want me?"

"You've got your choice, Cedar Lake or Elm Street."

"Cedar Lake. More traffic there."

"Roger."

Before he grabbed his tools, he heard a loud knock, then the doorbell. It was Giselle.

Chapter Five

After Giselle arrive, Cal clicked his phone off, climbed into his truck, and put it in gear. He cranked up the heat and defrost. Visibility sucked. He could see maybe ten feet in front of him. He proceeded slowly, keeping the vehicle at about twenty miles an hour.

While he drove, his mind roamed to Giselle. Her backing him up came as a surprise, but a welcome one. Maybe things between them had simmered down. They still had stuff to hash out. He had to explain why he got married and had Bobby. He supposed she still might be a tad pissed off.

After two dates with Jane, he'd stopped emailing Giselle. They'd been apart for five months and the communication had already petered off. Wracked with guilt about dating, he couldn't bear to write Giselle. He figured every email without mentioning Jane would be a lie. Although there wasn't much to tell, Jane had simply been a substitute for Giselle, a platonic substitute.

After more than a month, on their fifth date, two bottles of wine had taken platonic, ripped it up, and thrown it out the window. Hell, he was only human. Yep, they'd done the deed while riding a wine high. Of course, protection never entered his mind. He assumed every female was on the pill, if he even thought about it at all. His wine-addled brain had been shut down by his deprived dick.

After that night, Cal's guilt meter shot up to a thousand. He didn't call Jane, and he didn't write Giselle. Stuck in limbo, having done the wrong thing, he simply existed and tried like hell not to think about it.

But a phone call four weeks later shattered his world. Jane informed him he was going to be a father. Horrified, Cal took a week to mull over the situation. Then he did the right thing, even if his proposal wasn't exactly heartfelt.

"I think we should get married," he'd said, after Jane informed him she was keeping the baby.

He'd thrust a ring at her. Jane's reply had been snippy, and they'd argued.

"What the hell? I'm doin' the right thing here. I don't want my kid to grow up with only one parent. It's my kid, too. I should have a say."

"Real romantic," Jane sniffed.

"Come on, Jane. It's not like we've been dating for years. We barely know each other. But I'm willing to try being a family with you. Are you turning me down?"

She'd frowned. Cal knew she had options. They'd agreed to wait a month to think about it and continued dating. Jane had considered returning to California and moving in with her parents. Cal hated the idea. When Jane's folks died in a car crash, she agreed to marry Cal and start their family in Pine Grove. Her acceptance had been as half-hearted as his suggestion. When Jane started to show a little, they went to city hall and tied the knot.

He'd never told Giselle. Never told his parents the complete story, either. It had been a secret he'd shared with Jane. And now with her gone, it was his alone.

As he stared, squinting, into the snow, he decided Giselle had a right to know. She'd had a right all along, but he'd been too much of a coward to face her. The time had come. Since it happened a while ago, he figured she wouldn't be mad anymore. But you never knew with Giselle, never a predictable female. He tried to comfort himself she couldn't hurt him anymore, and she'd have to accept it as the truth.

Finally reaching his destination, he put the truck in Park, turned it off, donned gloves, and went out into the cold to see what needed to be done.

GISELLE HUNG UP THE phone. Panic shot through her. What did she know about taking care of a child? And in his house? Could she function? She wouldn't know where things were. She couldn't work his microwave.

"Get a grip. The boy needs you," she muttered to herself, digging out fleece pants. "You'll decide on the weather once you get out there." The idea maybe she could bring Bobby home calmed her. In her house, she could manage.

Shoving her feet in boots, she pulled her down jacket off the hook and bundled up. As she opened the door, the wind knocked her back. Damn! Could she hang on to Bobby against this vicious wind? Pushing forward, she lowered her head and trudged down the walk.

Sharp icy bits stung her face. She inhaled the frigid air in small breaths. Hunched over, she made slow progress toward Cal's house. There were no cars on the street, making crossing safe and easy. The cold cut through her clothes and froze her face, but she kept going because she'd promised Cal, and Bobby needed her.

Finally, she reached the entrance. Taking it slow, she gripped the wrought iron railing and took the steps one at a time. She gave a loud rap with her knuckles on the wooden door, and then rang the bell.

The knob turned, and the door opened. Giselle pushed her way inside.

"Thank you for coming. I've gotta run," Cal said, mussing his son's hair then brushing by her. In a flash, he was gone.

Giselle knelt down and drew the boy to her, hugging him.

"You're wet!"

"Oh! Yes. Sorry. Come on, let's get you dressed. Where is your snowsuit?"

"What's a snowsuit?"

"What do you wear out in the snow?"

"My snow pants and jacket."

Giselle struggled with the clothing, stopped, took a deep breath then started again.

"No. It goes this way," the boy said.

"Good. Help me, Bobby." When he was dressed, she said, "Come on. It's nasty out there, but we don't have far to go."

"Daddy said you were going to stay here with me."

"It's easier for me if I take you to my house. Okay?"

"But, Daddy..."

"Tell you what. After we get there, I'll call him and tell him where you are. How's that?"

"He's gonna be mad we didn't do what he said."

"Trust me. It's going to be okay."

She grasped his hand and opened the door. The wind gusted inside, assaulting their faces.

"I don't wanna go outside," the boy wailed.

"I'll make you hot chocolate when we get to my house."

At those magic words, Bobby stepped across the threshold and into the cold. They braved the winterish gusts from Mother Nature. Giselle kept a strong grip on his hand as the wind buffeted them about. When she felt him slipping, she reached over with her other hand. Together, they pushed through bluster and icy snow.

She'd left her door unlocked. After they climbed the slippery steps, sliding from side to side, she opened it quickly, pushing Bobby inside ahead of her. She shoved the door closed against the wind and let out a breath.

"We made it!" Bobby said.

"We did. Come on, let's get this wet stuff off and make that hot chocolate."

After the cocoa, Giselle pulled out a container of her homemade beef stew from the freezer and heated it up in the microwave. Bobby chowed down.

"This is good." He stabbed a potato with his fork.

Giselle smiled.

She served pound cake for dessert, and more hot chocolate, of course. After dinner, she cleaned up the dishes while Bobby drank a glass of milk.

"It's chilly in here. Darn wind! Seems like it's blowing through every crack in this house. Come on. We need a fire."

Within fifteen minutes, Giselle had stacked logs in the fireplace. She heated the chimney with newspaper to create a draft then shoved the burning paper under the logs. She'd practiced and could do it with ease. In a town where winter ruled, knowing how to light a fire was a necessity.

"That's a big fire," Bobby said as the flames shot up.

"I know. It's really cold today. We need a big one."

"Can we listen to the next chapter?"

"Sure."

Together, they moved the cushions off the sofa and arranged them in front of the fire. They added blankets and pillows from the bedrooms. Giselle stretched out and put the audiobook on. Bobby snuggled up to her. Within minutes, they were asleep. Giselle had forgotten to call Cal.

THERE WAS NOTHING LIKE working in the cold to take the stuffing out of you. By ten o'clock, exhaustion claimed Cal. He'd been sawing trees, moving chunks of trunks back and forth from the street to his truck. Working for hour after hour with no letup took all his energy. Bone cold and weary beyond belief, Cal hoped he could make it home without falling asleep at the wheel.

"You're full up, Cal. Why don't you knock off for tonight?" Dave said.

"I'm beat. I'll be back tomorrow."

"Thanks for your help."

The two men shook hands. There was only a little bit left to do on Cedar Lake Drive. Elm Street would have to wait, as would Grace Church. The electrical crew had to quit due to high winds. The weatherman said the storm would dissipate the next day and wind speed would drop back to about five miles an hour.

Beat to the soles of his feet, Cal climbed into his truck and steered the vehicle slowly home. Knowing he'd be sore as hell in the morning, he entered his house from the garage. Before undressing, he tiptoed into his son's room.

Not sure the lump in the bed was his boy or stuffed animals, he approached quietly. Bending down, he looked, but Bobby wasn't there. Panic seized him for a moment.

"They must be in the living room," he said.

Cal continued through the hall to the big room facing the front. But no Bobby. And no Giselle!

"What the hell? I told that boy not to leave the house." Now, panic grabbed him. His heart raced, adrenaline pumping through him.

"Where the hell could they be?"

He rubbed the back of his neck then peered out the front window. The street was quiet, not a car or a person to be seen. But wisps of smoke floated up from Giselle's chimney.

"Damn. She took him out in this blizzard? They must be there."

He set out in the cold one more time. Tramping through the deep snow, he skidded on the street and almost fell. Slowing his pace to secure his footing, he proceeded. Fear that her door was locked gave way when he turned the knob. It was open. Not exactly safe, but he was glad he could get in.

The crackle of a log on the fire drew his attention. The fire was the only light in the room. Pulling a flashlight out of his back pocket, he shone the beam on the living room. A big, blanket-covered lump lay on the floor in front of the fireplace.

Cal shucked his jacket and boots. Remembering he wore long johns, he took off his wet pants, too. He padded into the bathroom and looked for a place to hang his wet things, but Giselle's and Bobby's clothes took up the available spots. Feeling the garments, he took down the dry ones and substituted his in their place.

Returning to the living room, he stopped. Bobby had cuddled up to Giselle just like he did with his father. Cal's heart squeezed. They looked so natural together, so peaceful and content. She should have followed his orders, but no harm done.

A sudden chill swept through him. A cool draft washed over him. He approached the fire, gave it a good poke then added more logs. Bobby and Giselle hadn't left much room for another body, but he needed sleep.

Crouching down, he stretched out slowly, as not to disturb the others. He lifted the blankets and eased up flush with Giselle's back. Sliding his hand around her waist, he only disturbed her for a moment.

"Cal?"

"Yep."

She muttered something he couldn't understand and fell back to sleep. Bobby didn't budge. The heat from her body penetrated Cal, warming his bones. Damn it felt good to be lying next to her. They hadn't had a place to spend the night together before she left for Europe. He lived the dream as he bent to kiss her neck. Her sweet scent renewed old feelings. Damn, she smelled as good now as she had six years ago. Lovely Giselle, capable of breaking his heart with one stroke, would she do it again?

She didn't seem to mind having him against her. Since it might never happen again, he tried to seal the delicious memory in his mind forever, but exhaustion took its toll. His eyes fluttered closed, and he fell fast asleep.

"DADDY?"

Bobby's voice woke Giselle. The boy wiggled away from her and stood up. An arm around her waist came from behind, and when the boy scooted from underneath, it fell against her belly. *Cal? What's he doing here?* Groggy, she closed her eyes. Maybe this was a dream, and if she returned to slumber, it would continue.

Cal stirred then rolled over. His warm body moved away, allowing a chill to grip her. She pulled the blanket tighter.

"Wake up, Giselle." Bobby shook her.

She yawned and stretched. Cushions didn't help. Achy and stiff from sleeping on the floor, she stretched her arms up.

"Daddy's here. I'm hungry," Bobby said.

Slowly, she sat up. She rubbed her eyes, raised her arms above her head, and yawned again. "Okay. Give me a minute." Pushing to her knees then her feet, she stood. The house was cold. Wearing only leggings and a thin T-shirt, she wrapped her arms around her middle and shivered. "The fire's out."

"Can I have cereal?" Bobby asked.

"Sure. You get the box, I'll be there in a minute." Giselle padded into her room and grabbed a terry robe off the hook on the back of the door. She hoped Cal hadn't seen her in such revealing clothes. Nothing he hadn't seen before, but it had been a long time.

When she returned, he was up and sliding a leg into his pants.

"Sorry. It was late, and I was tired." He pulled his trousers up.

"No problem." Problem? She'd fought the instinct to snuggle into him with all she had. Still, waking up with Cal next to her had been a dream come true—for a brief moment.

Thank God he'd slept with a T-shirt on. No way could she have resisted touching him if he'd have been bare-chested. He gazed at her with sleepy eyes. Hair mussed, face scruffy, he looked like a refugee from a night of making love, not cleaning up after a storm.

At least that was what she thought. In all their young years together, and the times they'd made love, they had never spent an entire night together in a bed. They'd lived at home, with their parents. They had scoped out secret private spots in faraway fields, midnight at the lake, or the back of his old jalopy parked on a dead-end street for their trysts.

They had fallen in love anyway. Or so she'd thought.

"Giselle, you coming?" came the plaintive cry of a little boy.

"Excuse me." She tore herself away from watching him dress.

"I got the milk, too. But I can't reach the bowl," Bobby said.

Giselle smiled, and opened the cabinet door. "Here you go. Pour the cereal into the bowl."

She opened the milk carton. "Tell me when it's full, okay?"

"Okay."

While Bobby chowed down, she set up the coffeemaker. "Coffee?" she asked Cal.

"Thanks. I could use a cup. I have to get back. There's plenty left to do."

"Can I come?" Bobby asked.

"You've got school," Cal said. "I think."

Giselle flipped on the radio. The announcement of school closings came on, and, sure enough, Bobby's school was closed.

"Can I stay here?" he asked Giselle.

"If it's all right with your dad."

"Sure he won't be a bother?"

"No bother. I've stocked up on peanut butter, and we have a couple of chapters of the Hardy Boys book left."

"Thanks. It would help me out."

She smiled at him. When the machine finished brewing, Cal approached. She could feel his closeness, smell his scent. When he brushed by her, her skin tingled.

"Can I have toast, too?" Bobby asked.

"Sure. Cal?"

"Don't bother. I'll grab an egg sandwich from Java the Hut."

"It's no bother. I can add peanut butter, too."

"Peanut butter on toast? Yay!" Bobby said then finished his last spoonful of cereal.

"If you're gonna stay with Giselle, you have to listen to her and do exactly as she says. Her house, her rules."

"Okay."

"Can you get the bread for me, Bobby?"

The boy opened a drawer and pulled out a loaf. He brought it over to the toaster. "Can I put it in?"

"You can. Two slices for you and two for your dad."

"What about you?" the boy asked.

"Oh yes. Two for me, too."

She busied herself pulling down plates and retrieving a knife and the jar of peanut butter.

Cal filled two mugs with coffee. "One sugar and milk, right?"

"You remember?" she asked, stunned.

"Daddy, how did you know?"

She sensed heat rising to her face and turned away from them. She wondered if Cal was blushing, too.

"I met Giselle a long time ago. We went to high school together. Sort of. I was two years ahead of her. We were, uh, were...."

"Friends. We were friends," she put in.

"Yeah," Cal said.

Bobby seemed to take the news in stride. The toast popped up, and Giselle got to work. They sat at the small kitchen table and ate in peace. Giselle couldn't avoid Cal's gaze. While he appeared fuzzy to her, the heat from him radiated across the space.

Bobby ate quietly. Cal got up and poured his son a glass of milk.

"Thanks," Giselle said.

"I forgot how good toast is with peanut butter," Cal said.

"This is my first time," Bobby added.

"Giselle makes the best peanut butter toast, wouldn't you say, Bobby?" Cal asked.

The boy nodded.

Within a few minutes, Cal rose and loaded the dishes into the dishwasher. He wiped his son's mouth and hands.

"I brought some of Bobby's trucks over last night. Was that okay?"

"Of course," Cal replied. "You can go play, Son."

Bobby ran out of the room. The sound of him crashing his vehicles together met her ears.

"Thanks so much for bringing him here."

"I know you said not to go out. But it was much easier to have him here."

"Whatever works. I'm sorry about joining you."

"Are you? I'm not," she said, her voice small.

CAL DIDN'T KNOW WHAT to say. He wanted to kiss her but held back. Surprised she wasn't mad when she woke up and found him glued to her backside, Cal hoped this meant a truce. But it wouldn't be enough. Calling a halt to hostilities would be a beginning. He wanted more, much more. He wanted to start over and rebuild what they once had—if it was possible.

She walked him to the door and hesitated. It reminded him of days past, when she'd linger at the front door of her house, waiting for him to kiss her. With mischief in mind, he'd string her along, drawing it out, until she almost slammed inside the house, before he took her in his arms.

Could they wind the clock back or start over? He'd changed in the last six years, had she? Of course, people didn't stand still. But their core values didn't change. Giselle always liked kids. One of her traits that made him believe she'd be a good mother someday. Her kindness to his son touched Cal's heart. The boy adored her.

He sighed as he picked up his jacket.

"Is there a lot left to do?"

"My parents are trapped. Time to remove the tree blocking Grace Church Street."

"I hope they're all right."

Cal chuckled. "My dad told me not to hurry. He said Mom was baking his favorite cookies."

Giselle laughed.

"Bobby sure likes it here. I'd swear you have a circus or something hiding in the back."

"Nope. Just toys, books, and food."

Cal cupped her cheek, running his thumb over her soft skin before he zipped up and headed out. He looked back to see her standing in the doorway, her robe belted tight, her hand raised in a single wave. Wouldn't it be great to see her beautiful smiling face every morning?

The air was cold but clear. No clouds, but the winter sun didn't bring much heat. He climbed into his truck and steered toward Grace Church. He picked up the radio. "Dave, I'm on my way." He steered through the plowed streets with ease.

"Good timing. The electrical people arrived an hour ago and secured the wires."

When he got to the street, he unloaded his chain saw, and approached the tree. A huge pine sprawled across the pavement. It had knocked down wires and a mailbox on its way over. The Con Ed truck had parked on the side of the road. A man on a ladder, finished fooling with the wire, put his tools in a box, and started down.

Several cars turned around. A few waited. Cal waved and switched on the saw. He started at the thin end, knowing he could open one lane right away.

"Dave, I'll clear this out. You direct traffic," Cal said.

Progress took time. The sky had been overcast when he drove up, now darker clouds rolled in, thickening the air and threatening. Wind picked up. Cal focused hard, working faster. Changing weather conditions might stop him in his tracks.

Dave waved cars through a few at a time. When the temperature dropped, Cal rubbed his hands together to keep his fingers from freezing. He didn't wear gloves with the electric saw because he needed a firm grip. And, hell, no man wanted a ferocious cutting machine to slip.

He flipped the collar of his jacket up and increased his work speed. He'd cleared three quarters of the road. All he had left was the most massive part of the trunk. Cal continued cutting off the limbs, which were getting bigger and thicker as he moved down the trunk.

The street had not been plowed. Trudging through the snow and ice to carry the limbs to his truck slowed him down, tired him out. One minute he was walking, and the next he was sliding. When Cal approached the remaining trunk and branches, he lost his footing, and slid toward the open lane. A car zoomed through, speeding, and collided with him. Cal bounced off the vehicle, crashing into the tree trunk and caromed off.

His hands flailed, reaching for anything to break his fall. His right gripped a limb stump, but his speed kept him going, the rough bark ripping the skin from his palm. Pine needles scratched his face as he fell, backwards. His head hit the pavement. Pain seared through him then everything went black.

Chapter Six

The wail of a siren caught Giselle's attention. She shuddered to think what might have happened to someone in the aftermath of this storm. They didn't have many serious emergencies in Pine Grove.

She and Bobby had finished lunch. They had replenished the fire with fresh logs and lay down on the cushions near the warmth for a nap. Bobby fell asleep first.

Her cell rang. Giselle took it into the kitchen.

"Hi, it's me, Betty. Cal's mom."

"Hi, Betty. What's up?"

"Cal got hurt today. He's not critical or anything, but he's a little ripped up and got a concussion."

"Oh my God. Is he all right?"

"He's gonna be fine. But he needs quiet and rest for a while."

"Where are you?"

"At Oak Bend General Hospital."

"Oh my God." Giselle sank down on a chair.

"He'll be coming home in a couple of hours. They want to do some tests. Might keep him overnight, but I doubt it. At least he got our street open. I'm coming to take Bobby off your hands."

"He's no trouble."

"I know. But he needs to know about his father. See him. Know he's going to be okay. We'll keep him for a week while Cal recuperates at home."

"They'll be separated?"

"It's best for Cal to have peace and quiet. I'll make some casseroles. We love having Bobby."

"I've enjoyed his company."

"He adores you. It's so wonderful that you took him so Cal could help with the cleanup."

"Just being neighborly."

Betty laughed. "I doubt it was just that. I'm sure it wasn't easy for you, in your condition."

"You know?"

"Laura Dailey told me."

"Then everyone in town must know."

"No one's told Cal. You've asked us not to, and while I don't agree, personally, we've all honored your wishes."

"I don't want pity from him. I'm fine. I get around, get everything done. It may take me a little longer to do some things, but they get done."

"I know. I'm so proud of you. Your mother would have been, too. You're self-sufficient. I hope you'll tell him. And soon."

"Why?"

"He knows something's up. He was fishing for answers from me, but I dodged him."

"I appreciate it."

"It's hard to avoid his questions."

"I'll tell him. Soon."

"If there's anything I can do for you, just call. You've always been like a daughter to me."

"Thank you, Betty. I feel the same about you. But it's awkward now. You know."

"Push the old stuff aside and don't be a stranger."

Emotion choked Giselle. "I miss my mom so much."

"I'm sure you do, sweetheart. I heard your aunt Julia is planning a trip to New York City for Christmas. Why don't you spend it with us?"

"That's very kind. I'm not there yet."

"Okay, then. But I'll be helping you in the thrift shop."

"Great."

Giselle put the phone down. She loved Cal's parents. They had always been kind to her. Betty had confided she wanted her for her daughter-in-law. But circumstances had thrown a wrench into those plans. After hearing about Cal's marriage, Giselle had renewed her contract with Saucier, Inc. and continued her work designing office space in Europe.

No way could she return to Pine Grove. Seeing Cal and his wife—simply thinking the words "Cal's wife" upset her stomach. Even after Jane died, Giselle couldn't return home. Only after her disability prevented her from working, and her father passed, did she realize the only place she could be was Pine Grove.

She sought the familiar. After selling her folks' home, she had a substantial nest egg. She could have lived anywhere but chose to remain in her hometown. Knowing she'd need help with getting around, chopping wood, and various chores, she counted on the goodwill and friendly attitude of her neighbors.

Giselle prepared another pot of hot chocolate and left it simmering on the stove while she gathered Bobby's things. The little boy brought a happy spirit to her home. He'd lit up her house with laughter and fun. She'd miss him.

Watching out the window, she sipped the warm drink. A car pulled up. Betty got out.

"So good to see you. You look wonderful," Betty said, hugging Giselle.

"Bobby's still asleep. Would you like some hot chocolate or coffee?"

"Oooh. Hot chocolate?"

"My special flavor."

The women sat in the kitchen and chatted about the thrift shop until Bobby awoke. He wandered in, rubbing his eyes.

"Here you go." Giselle set a mug of the beverage on the table.

"What's Grandma doing here?"

"You're going to come stay with me for a week," Betty said.

"Where's Dad?"

"I'll take you to see him as soon as you finish up here." Betty washed out her empty cup.

Bobby drank while his grandma packed his things.

"Soon?" Betty asked, zipping up her jacket.

"Soon," Giselle responded.

Standing in the doorway, she watched Betty put the boy in his car seat and then drive away. The open door cooled the house. She put more logs on the fire, wrapped herself in a blanket, and sat, cross-legged, in front of the blaze. Betty had been right. Giselle had to tell Cal. It would be better coming from her. But he was injured now, so this might not be a good time.

She sighed. Her phone rang.

"Hi, Chris."

"Just calling to say we're snowed in here. But I'll be by to get you tomorrow morning. Okay?"

"Perfect. Thanks."

Giselle took a deep breath. *Time to get Santa's Thrift Shop up and running. And figure out a way to tell Cal the truth.*

"BUT I FEEL FINE," CAL protested.

"Sure you do, but your brain doesn't. Stick to the rules, Cal. Rest. Off your feet. No TV, no reading, no exercise of any kind. I want you calm, in bed, sleeping, staring out the window."

"Can I eat?"

The doctor shot him a sharp glance. "Don't joke. A concussion is no laughing matter."

"Okay, okay. I get it."

"Oh, and by the way, no sex."

Cal laughed. "That won't be a problem."

"Oh? Too bad. But maybe it's good. At least for this week."

"Don't worry about the sex part for next week, doc. There's nothing on the horizon."

The doctor patted him on the arm. "I hope things pick up in that department, Cal."

"When pigs can fly. For now, Bobby's staying with my parents."

"Perfect. Next week, you can walk him to school and pick him up. Mild exercise will be okay. For next week. Not this week. No driving this week, either."

"I might as well be dead."

"You can listen to books on audio or the radio."

"Gee, thanks."

"Stuff the sarcasm. This is for your own good. And for Bobby's."

"Right. I have to think about him."

"Buy prepared foods. Get your mom to cook for you. Take it easy. I want you in here next Monday for tests before I give you the go-ahead for more activity."

The doctor gave him a prescription for vitamins and a pamphlet on concussions. A nurse rolled Cal out to the curb in a wheelchair. He got in the front seat with his dad. When his shoulder hit the seat, he groaned.

"Shoulder bothering you?"

"I landed there first. Guess that's lucky. Might have done me in for my head to hit first."

"Damn! That was some accident."

Cal examined his bandaged hand. "It'll heal. Just take some time."

"Doc put you on bed rest?" His father backed out of the lot.

"Practically."

"We're happy to have Bobby for the week."

"Thanks. Rest is impossible when he's around." Cal chuckled.

"He's sure a lively boy. He talks a lot about Giselle. Do you think it's wise to let him get so attached to her?"

"What can I do about it? Forbid him to go there?"

"Well, I mean with her situation, and all."

"Her what? What situation? She lives across the street." Cal cocked an eyebrow.

His father coughed, blushed a little, and remained silent.

"Is there something going on? Something I should know about?"

"I don't think so," his father responded, but wouldn't look him in the eye.

"Something's fishy. She's not an axe murderer. Not that I know."

"No, no, nothing like that. I just mean. Well, you're not seeing her. And...well, to be blunt, the boy needs a mother," Al Morrison said.

"Agreed. How do I find one? Put an ad on Craigslist? Adorable little boy seeks mom?"

"If he gets too attached to her... What if she hooks up with someone else?"

"Or, like, marries someone?'

"Yeah."

"Nothing I can do about it." Cal compressed his lips into a thin line.

"Damn it, Son. There is something you can do!"

"What?"

"Do I have to spell it out for you? Marry her yourself!"

Cal laughed. "I think the lady has to be willing. She hates me."

"I doubt that."

"We've had a few words. She's done with me. Was when she left, I was too stupid to see it."

"I disagree. If she has the type of relationship with Bobby that he talks about, well, seems to me it's her way of getting to you."

"You think she's manipulating the boy to get to the man?" Cal asked, his eyes wide.

"I don't think so. But it seems like that's what she's doing. With good intent, not bad. Like she sees you in him and she responds. Or some such nonsense."

"Oh, I see what you mean. No. I don't think she misses me."

He father shrugged. "Suit yourself. If you want to be blind, I can't stop you."

"You think she has feelings for me?"

"Of course. Why else would she be so close to your son? Your concussion has affected your brain." His dad shook his head. "You'd better rest. You're worse off than I thought." He pulled up in front of Cal's house. "Doc said you can't carry these. I'll do it." Al Morrison picked up two shopping bags loaded with food. "Your mother said to call her if you need anything. She'll stop at the store and run it over to you."

The men chatted as they made their way up the walk and into Cal's house.

"This looks like enough to feed all of Pine Grove for a month. I'll be fine," Cal said.

"The little waitress over at Java the Hut used to have a thing for you. Maybe she'd deliver some food if you need it."

"Don't get any ideas, Pop."

"It's not me. It's her."

"Doc said no sex this week, either."

He father laughed as he blushed. "Well, maybe you'd better call your mother or me instead."

The men hugged. Cal walked his father to the door. He stopped on the stoop and stared across the street. Giselle appeared in the window and waved at him. He waved back. *Damn. Right across the street, so pretty, so sweet.*

He'd never admit it, but the stay in the hospital, the doctor's visit, and the trip home had tired him. Cal toed off his shoes and stretched out on the sofa. He covered himself with a throw and scrunched up a couple of pillows behind his head. Maybe he couldn't have sex this week, but he could dream about it. He closed his eyes and remembered the night he spent curled up around Giselle, behind her in front of the fire. Ah, sweet.

AS SHE WATCHED AL MORRISON'S car drive away, Giselle sighed. She sank back onto the sofa. When Betty had called, the news stunned her. Neither woman let her fear show in front of Bobby. But Betty never called her to give her an update. She'd called the hospital, but they wouldn't tell her anything. She couldn't reach Betty, either. Giselle was up half the night, worrying about Cal.

Now he was home, so he must be okay. She took a deep breath and stared out the window. Why did she worry about a man who didn't care a lick for her? It's not like he would have worried about her if the situation had been reversed. Still, he had been out cold and now probably had to rest. Telling Cal to rest was like trying to tether a cheetah. Restless, always moving, Cal was a very physical man. He was probably losing his mind.

She padded into the kitchen and set about making her signature brownies. Nothing like chocolate brownies to cheer a person up. She'd made them for him several times in high school. Once, he got banged up pretty bad playing football. She'd whipped up a batch and delivered them. She'd read to him then, too, from one of her favorite books—*Catcher in the Rye.*

With flashlight and magnifying glass on the counter, Giselle was able to decipher the instructions well enough to get the batter mixed. She slid the pan into the oven and turned on her talking timer. Then she lay down on the sofa and turned on an audiobook. Before long, she'd dozed off. The loud voice of the timer startled her awake. Yawning, she took the brownies out of the oven and put them on the window sill to cool.

She pulled on leggings and her favorite flannel shirt. After packing up the sweets, she yanked on boots and trudged slowly across the street. The bright whiteness of the snow reflected light, helping her to see her way. Butterflies jumped in her belly as she pushed the bell at Cal's place.

The wind whipped around her legs with icy fingers. She shivered as she waited. What was taking so long? Finally, the door opened. There he stood in jeans and a T-shirt, rubbing his face and yawning. Turning her head slightly, she saw tousled hair and a handsome face darkened with several days of scruff. God, he looked gorgeous.

"I brought these for you."

"Your brownies?"

She nodded.

"Damn. I used to love those."

"Are you okay?" she said, trying to stop shaking.

"Yeah, yeah. A concussion, bruised shoulder. I'm fine."

Silence.

"Good. Well. Then, I'll be getting back," she said, turning. Wasn't he going to invite her in?

"No, no. Wait. I'm sorry. I was asleep. Come in, come in." He grasped her elbow.

"I woke you up? I'm so sorry. I should leave and let you get back to bed."

"Come on in. At least have a brownie with me." He pulled her in and shut the door.

The warmth of the room enveloped her.

"Let me put these in the kitchen," he said, disappearing.

Giselle smelled the fire in the fireplace. She made her way slowly there to chase the frostiness from her hands.

"I fell asleep with the fire burning the other day. Do you think it's safe??"

"I don't worry about it," he said, joining her. "There's a screen and nothing flammable nearby. You should get a screen. And a fire extinguisher. Sit down." He ushered her toward his sofa. It was a big sectional in front of the fireplace. There was a television on the side.

When the couch hit the backs of her knees, she sat down abruptly.

"You okay?" Cal asked.

"Fine."

"Want some coffee or a glass of milk with the brownie?"

"Milk would be great. Thanks."

"Stay here. I'll bring it out."

"Should you be doing this?" she asked.

"I'm not an invalid. I need to rest up some."

"Waiting on me isn't resting."

"Don't worry about it. It's fine." He left and returned carrying a tray. He set it on the coffee table. Giselle's nerves kicked up. Could she handle things without giving away her sight restriction?

"I'm not really thirsty. Just a brownie."

"Suit yourself," he replied.

She managed to distinguish the plate of dark food and plucked one off. She took a bite.

"These are just as good as the ones you made in high school."

"Thanks."

They ate in silence. Cal sat close to her. Heat radiated from him. His leg pressed against her thigh for a moment, kicking up a totally different emotion. She chewed and swallowed quickly then pushed to her feet.

"Time to go. Let you rest. If you need anything, I'm just across the street."

"Thanks."

"Do you have my cell?"

"I think so." He reached over, grabbed his phone then rattled off the number his mother had given him.

"That's it. Call me if you need me."

"Thanks."

They walked to the door together. Giselle stumbled over the leg of a chair. Cal caught her.

"Whoa! Hey, you okay?"

"Fine. Just clumsy," she said, trying to smile. For a moment, she caught his masculine scent, and her cheek brushed the softness of his shirt. Her face rested against his chest. Damn, his muscles were as hard as they had been years ago. His arms held her tight, trapping her against him. She allowed her eyes to drift shut for a moment, enjoying his closeness.

"Uh," he uttered and stopped. "Thanks for the brownies."

"Oh yes. Pardon me. Time to go." She pushed off but enjoyed the feel of his chest under her palms. Goodbyes were said, and she was out in the bitter cold, bending her head against the unforgiving wind. With arms wrapped around her torso, she trudged through the snow until she reached her front steps. Gripping the handrail, Giselle climbed slowly and opened the door.

Once inside, she dressed down and lit a fire. Wrapped in a blanket, she curled up on the sofa, hugging a pillow to her chest and wishing with all her might it was Cal Morrison instead.

IT WAS A MIRACLE CAL still had a few brownies left the next morning. As he lay on the sofa, munching on one and nursing a cup of coffee, the black Bentley drove up and parked in front of Giselle's house. Damn it! She came out in leggings and a down coat. He could tell from the way she walked she was cold. The man behind the wheel got out and held the door.

"Ass-kisser," Cal mumbled.

Giselle smiled at the man and got in the front seat. This was the fourth day in a row this asshole had picked her up. Cal didn't like it. This guy was making time with Giselle. Didn't he know she belonged to Cal? He was always at the window when the creep brought her home.

At least he didn't spend the night, which would have been more than Cal could stomach.

As the car drove away, Cal checked his watch. He frowned. She'd better be back by lunchtime. Or what was he going to do about it? He shook his head then padded into the kitchen for a refill. There was nothing he could do about it. She didn't belong to him, though he refused to admit it. However, her trip to visit him and drop off brownies meant something. Damned if he could figure out what.

Sick and tired of resting, he swore the inactivity made him more nervous than relaxed. Cal returned to the living room. He put his mug down and paced. He rotated his arm, wincing at the pain from his shoulder.

"Dammit, I feel fine," he said, picking up the remote for the television. After zooming through all the stations and discovering there was nothing worth watching, he yanked on long johns and his down jacket then headed for the garage. Picking up a snow shovel, he muttered to himself.

"Someone's gonna get killed on my walk. I'm good with this." He went outside. Careful not to use his injured shoulder much, he scraped the implement along the stone, lifting off a two-inch base of ice and slush.

His head cleared, his lungs filled with fresh air. Feeling normal, Cal almost didn't notice the Bentley pull up to drop off Giselle. He stopped and leaned on the handle, watching her get out. At least she didn't kiss the guy. If she had, Cal might've had to punch him out. And with a bad shoulder, it wouldn't have been the brightest idea.

When she shut the door, he went back to shoveling.

"Hey!" Cal kept his head down, shoveled the edge under the ice then tossed it aside.

"Hey! You!"

Again, he ignored her. Couldn't be talking to him.

"Hey, you, Cal. With the thick head!"

That got his attention. He raised his gaze to Giselle's. She stood in the street, yelling.

"You are one stubborn man."

"Me? I'm not stupid enough to be standing in the street," he replied.

"You're not supposed to be doing this."

"And you're not supposed to be in the way of moving vehicles."

"Where?" She turned her head from side to side.

"Nobody's coming...yet."

"Didn't the doctor tell you not to do that?"

"So? I'm feeling fine."

"And your shoulder?"

"It's a little stiff."

"Idiot!"

"Who you calling an idiot?"

"You! Go ahead, don't listen to the doctor. Screw up your brain, if you still have one. Reinjure your shoulder so you can't work. What a dumb thing to do."

Her face grew pink as she gestured with her hands, but she got so caught up in her tirade, she didn't see a car coming. Cal did. He dropped the shovel and leaped into the air. He caught her on the fly, tackling her, falling to the ground, and ending up a whisker away from the road.

The oncoming car hit the brakes and skidded. Cal clasped Giselle tight, rolling them over and over until they were safe. The car stopped abruptly. The driver opened his window.

"Hey, lady, whatcha doin' standin' in the street? Idiot!" He frowned and went on his way.

Lying next to her, Cal pushed up on his elbow. Giselle's face and hair were covered with snow. She coughed and pushed the slushy mess from her mouth.

"What did you do?" she asked, sputtering.

"Saved your sorry ass."

She stilled, staring at him.

"Damn car almost skidded right over us, or didn't you notice?"

She caught her breath and covered her mouth. "Really?" she whispered.

"You didn't see it, did you?"

She shook her head.

"Too busy telling me off?"

She nodded.

Cal gave a mirthless laugh. "Just like you."

"Thank you for saving me."

He brushed snow off her hair then ran a gloved finger down her cheek. The cold gave her skin a healthy pinkish glow. Remnants of lipstick stained her lips a soft, inviting coral shade. A few reddish strands in her bangs glinted in the sunlight peeking out from behind a cloud.

Cal bent down and kissed her.

Chapter Seven

The next morning, when the Bentley drove off, Cal tore himself away from the window. He pulled his robe tighter and lay back on the sofa. Damned if he'd admit it, but the escapade outside had tired him. He shut his eyes and focused on the feeling of that amazing kiss.

His cell phone woke him up.

"Radio says school's back tomorrow," Cal's father said.

Cal completed a yawn before responding. "Good. Can you take him? I'll pick him up."

"Are you sure you're up to it?"

"Should be plowed. No problem. Thanks, Pop. And thank Ma, too, will ya?"

"Sure will. We're going to miss Bobby. He's a great kid. Guess you'll be glad to get him back."

"Yep. Too damn quiet around here."

Cal put the phone down and padded into the kitchen. It was lunchtime. He prepared a sandwich. When he heard the sound of a door closing, he ran to the window. There she was, getting out of the Bentley again, right on schedule. Home every day for lunch. Whew, she didn't invite him in. Cal took a deep breath.

Damn, how long could he keep this up? Desire grew in him daily. Tamping it down had worked for a while but wore thin. And the kiss. She didn't resist. What the hell was he waiting for?

His life wasn't just about him, he had Bobby to consider. The kid had taken to Giselle as if she was his mother. Cal apologized to the air for even having that thought. Jane had been an amazing mother. Cal likened Bobby's even temperament to Jane, her genes, and her influence. No one had ever accused Cal of being mild-mannered.

If Bobby liked Giselle, how did she feel about him? He couldn't bring a woman into his small family who didn't love his son, and would treat him as her own. He vowed to pay more attention to her when Bobby was around. He'd evaluate the situation before he made a move on her. Never too late to tread lightly before he jumped in. His mother would be proud. She'd been pounding that lesson into his head since he was five. Guess it finally took.

His father had been right. Cal missed his son. The little bundle of energy who kept him running owned Cal. He'd never had love like that. It gripped his heart and wouldn't let go.

He finished his sandwich and downed a glass of milk. He'd been listening to one of those audiobooks Giselle had given him before he had to go out and shovel snow. Now, he resumed his position on the couch and flipped the sound back on.

He tried to focus on the story, but, before he knew it, he'd fallen asleep. When he awoke, there were shadows on the front lawn. The sun had almost set. Shortest day of the year would be here before he knew it. He sighed. Last night without his boy. Cal heated up leftovers and broke the rules, turning on his computer and watching an X-rated movie.

The moment a naked woman appeared on the screen, his mind zipped back to the first time he'd seen Giselle naked. She'd been shy, not about letting him touch her, but about shedding her clothes. They'd been skinny-dipping in the lake a couple of times, but she'd made him turn around before she slipped off her bathing suit.

He stopped the movie, closed his eyes, and relived that special night.

"Do I have to turn around?" he'd whined.

She shook her head.

"Really? You're going to get undressed in front of me?"

"Only if you do, too," she'd whispered.

He'd pushed down his trunks in a heartbeat. "Now you," he said, sitting on the edge of the dock, his feet dangling over. He wanted a good seat to watch this strip show.

"Okay," she said, her voice shaking.

She pushed to her feet and reached around behind her to unhook her top. Cal couldn't believe he got hard from simply watching her. She slipped it off, exposing the nicest breasts he'd ever seen. And, yeah, at nineteen, he'd seen a few pair.

"You're staring," she'd said.

"Sorry," he mumbled and looked away for a moment.

She closed her fingers over the edges of her bikini bottoms and shoved them down then stepped out. "There. Happy?" she asked, her hands on her hips, her face in shadow.

The way the moonlight shone down on her leaving sexy shadows and shading her luscious curves, Cal feared he'd come on the spot.

"You're the most beautiful woman I've ever seen. Bar none. No magazine, no movie. Nothing compares to you, Zell."

"Really?"

He'd patted the wood plank next to him. "Come here."

She'd tiptoed along and sat next to him. He didn't know where to touch her first.

"Last one in's a rotten egg." She'd slipped into the water before he could make a move.

Cal had laughed and followed her. They swam out to the floating dock and made love. He'd never had a woman that way before. Even remembering intoxicated him. He wanted her, he needed her. And this no-sex thing would have to go. Cal switched off the computer and headed for the shower. He needed to relieve himself, doctor's orders or not.

THE NEXT DAY, THE SUN shined bright, melting the snow and ice. Chris showed up at nine and whisked Giselle away to the shop. She put on Christmas music and soaped up a sponge. Shelves, counters, and tables needed to be scrubbed.

Jory, Mindy, and Jess would arrive soon to create merchandise displays. Once she finished washing, Giselle returned to sorting the donations. She had men's, women's, sister's, and brother's goods piled in boxes, on tables, and in bags. Time to organize the clothes, books, and toys.

With Christmas only a few weeks away, the place had to be ready for "shoppers," as she called them. Jess set up a schedule of group visitors and printed in large black letters and numbers on a white board. The contrast made it easier for Giselle to read. Children would be coming through every morning for the next week.

She'd be in the shop all day, dealing with the kids in the morning and straightening up and arranging for the groups coming the next day in the afternoon. Humming as she worked, she thought about a gift for Bobby. Of course, Cal would object, but she didn't care. They had a rapport, and she wanted to get him something. He'd talked about a Lego firehouse. With help from her friends, she'd ordered it online.

Chris had helped her tote boxes of books. In the shop, she fingered her family's Christmas tree ornaments. They lay carefully displayed in a box on a table. The little girl frog on skis, the red ball with a gold glitter design, the matching balls in silver and gold with blue or white intricate designs nestled in tissue paper, awaiting new homes.

Julia had asked about a Christmas tree, but Giselle had nixed the idea.

"Too many problems. Little things can fall and break, leaving glass on the floor I might miss. How could I find everything to take down after the holidays? Too much stress."

Giselle missed the scent of fresh pine she associated with the chilly, snowy weather, but she'd made up her mind. Many things had changed, except her feelings for Cal Morrison. Watching him with his son, her heart swelled. He had become the father she had envisioned when they were dating.

When he turned twenty, Cal matured. His father had had an accident, and Cal had to take over the tree business for six months. Responsible, grounded, and in love with her, Cal made it hard for her to leave.

Giselle pushed away the ornament box. No sense crying over what was. She had to deal with what is—and that was enough.

"Rockin' Around the Christmas Tree" came on the radio, lifting her spirits. She smiled and danced around the room, singing along. The bell over the door tinkled.

"Santa's helpers have arrived," said Jory, opening the door.

"*Entrez,* my friends. *Entrez*!"

Jory and Mindy raised their voices in song as they folded garments, wiped down toys and gadgets, and set things in their proper place, under Giselle's direction. The store shelves, stuffed with clothing, toys, and books invited browsing.

"Do you think we have enough stuff?"

"This is at least twice what your mom had," Jory said.

"Maybe three times," Mindy put in.

"Good. Then we'll have some leftover to sell and maybe be able to pay the taxes for this pathetic building."

"Isn't it in good shape?" Jory grabbed a spare chair.

"I haven't checked. Not that I would know if it is or isn't."

"I mean, you'd notice if the foundation was crumbling, right?" Mindy asked.

"I'd have to get right down there with a magnifying glass."

The women nodded.

"I'll have to have someone check it out. It should be inspected, I think. Isn't that the law?"

"I have no clue. Trent takes care of that stuff," Jory said.

"Maybe for fire?" Mindy asked. "The firemen come around about once a year to check out the theater. And I know I need to have my sprinkler system checked regularly."

"Sprinkler system. Damn. I don't even know if we have one," Giselle said.

"There's a hunky new volunteer guy in the firehouse. I think his name is Flint."

"What a sexy name!" Giselle clasped her hands together in front of her chest.

"We'll take you over there when we finish here," Jory said. "It's about time you met some of the new guys in Pine Grove."

"And stop thinking about Cal," Mindy admonished.

"Wish I could," Giselle muttered.

CAL AWOKE WITH A HEADACHE. He went back to sleep, rising with the beep of the alarm clock half an hour before pickup time. The temperature had warmed to a balmy thirty degrees. He yanked on his boots, shrugged on his down jacket, and headed to school to pick up Bobby.

The boy came flying out of the brick building, first child out the door, and right into his father's arms. His leap was so powerful, he almost knocked Cal over.

"Hey, buddy."

"Daddy!" Bobby snuggled his face in his father's jacket.

"Sure missed you. Sure did," Cal muttered, stroking his son's head.

"Me, too!" He stretched his arms as wide as they would go but still couldn't get them completely around his father's shoulders. Cal lifted his son in arms and carried him home.

The boy babbled all the way. Cal simply muttered "uh-huh," and "yes, right," from time to time as he walked. Bobby's noisy warmth cheered him. Cal grinned all the way home.

When they arrived and shed their snow gear, Bobby ran to the kitchen.

"I'm hungry."

"Wait a sec," Cal said, hitting forty-five seconds on the microwave. When it was done, he took out a mug of hot chocolate and placed it on the table next to a small bowl of pretzels and a plate of orange sections. Bobby dug into his snack. Cal heated some cocoa for himself.

"What did you learn in school today?" Cal sipped the hot liquid.

Bobby gave him a rundown on every project.

"And we have to do this. We have to make a dio-something."

"Diorama?" Cal said.

The boy nodded. "A circus and we have to find animals in magazines or online and cut out the pictures and write the animal's name. Then we have to learn where he lives and what he eats and stuff."

Cal searched Bobby's backpack and found a piece of paper outlining the project. Damn it. Although he was better, his head pounded. He stretched out on the sofa while Bobby turned on the television. Cal shut his eyes.

"I'm afraid I can't help you with your project," Cal said.

"Why not?"

"My head's not back to normal yet. I'd like to, but I'm not supposed to do that kind of thing. No computer work. No concentration."

Bobby kissed his father's cheek and stroked his hair.

Cal chuckled. "I'm okay. Mostly. But I need another week of rest."

Bobby started to cry.

"I'm okay, Son. No need for that." Cal sat up.

"Who's going to help me with my dio-thing?"

At that moment, Giselle came out of her house, heading for the mailbox. The movement of her against the snow drew Cal's eye.

"How about Giselle? Do you think it's something she could do?"

"Can I go and ask her?"

"Yep. She's outside right now. Get your jacket," Cal said, rising to his feet.

He hated stupid effing art projects from Bobby's school. Now he'd have to find a shoebox, buy glue and a lot of other crap they'd never use again.

A smug smile spread across his face. Yeah, let Miss Goody Goody do it. She made him hot chocolate, bandaged a skinned knee, took him in when Cal had an emergency. The boy thought the sun rose in her. Let her deal with this shit.

Cal zipped up the boy's jacket and he was out the door in a flash. Cal stood by the window, chuckling to himself how he'd foisted off this unwanted project on her. Did he feel guilty? Not one little bit. She was home. Hell, she was always home. He watched Bobby go inside then stepped into the kitchen to prepare dinner.

He put water on to boil for spaghetti when the door opened.

"Giselle said she can't do it," Bobby moaned, slumping down on a chair at the table.

"What?" Cal faced his son.

"Yeah. That's what she said."

Was this what people meant by "fair-weather friend"? She'd crapped out on him and now his son, too. Counting on her had been a mistake. He was a fool to think she'd take over for him, even though he could never do a decent job, and she could do it blindfolded. Can't do it? Doesn't want to do it is more like it. He totally got that.

"She said she was sorry. Awful sorry."

"I bet." Cal's lips compressed into a thin line. "I'll talk to her," he said, sloughing his coat over his shoulders.

"Dad!"

"It's okay, Son. I'm just going to talk to her." Cal knelt down to be eye to eye with Bobby.

"Be nice. Okay?"

"Okay," Cal said, smiling. He turned a movie on the television and handed his boy a small bag of pretzels and a juice box. "I'll be home soon."

Bobby nodded, his attention already on the television set.

As Cal opened the door, he marveled at the compassionate, sweet nature of his son. Would some woman come along and take advantage of the boy someday? Probably, just like Giselle had taken Cal for a ride. The grin melted off his face as he strode across the frozen grass and up her walkway. He rapped on the door.

"Yes?" she called through the door.

"It's me. Cal."

"Of course. Door's open, come in."

As he entered the house, the smell of something cinnamon met his nose. His stomach rumbled.

"Would you like a cinnamon bun? Bobby had one when he was here. I hope that's all right."

Anger fought with his stomach. How could he eat her baked goods and yell at her at the same time? He drew on his inner strength.

"No. That's not what I came for."

"Oh? Then what?"

He shifted his weight and cleared this throat. "Bobby said you turned him down."

"What?" She moved toward the kitchen and he followed.

"He asked you for help on his school project and you said 'no.' Is that right?"

"Yes."

"You know I'm no good at art. But you are."

"You sent him over to ask me?" She faced him.

"I did. I thought you were his friend." Cal rested his hands on his hips.

"I am his friend."

"You told him you can't do it."

"Right. I can't."

"Really? Not exactly what one friend says to another. You're leaving him high and dry."

"I can't help it. I can't do it." Her face flushed as she turned away from him.

He grabbed her arm and twirled around to face him. "What the hell? You might hate me but don't take it out on my son! Damn it, Giselle, what's going on?" His voice rose as the words spilled from his lips.

TURNING AWAY WOULDN'T help. The moment had come for Giselle to tell Cal the truth. Face-to-face, she cringed at the waves of his rage coming her way. *Does he hate me that much?* Tears stung, but she forced them back.

"You said you can't do it. Why?" he demanded, his face stormy, his brows drawn together.

"Because I can't. Won't you just accept that?" she pleaded, hoping he'd let it go and she could continue to keep her secret.

"No! Damn it! I won't. It's not about me. It's about Bobby. There's one little boy in my house, brooding, sad, because his friend shut him down. You deserted him. He's hurtin' and it's not okay!"

At his yelling, she backed away.

"Please stop yelling!" She sounded braver than she felt.

Her words stopped him. He paused, staring at her. The heat went out of him, replaced by a look of confusion and hurt.

"Did you think I was going to hit you?"

"No, but you're a different man from the one I knew six years ago."

"No, I'm not. I'd never hit you. I don't hit women."

She blew out a breath. He took a deep breath. "All I want is a straight answer," he said, his voice quieter.

"I gave you the only answer I can."

"I don't believe you. You're a bad liar, Giselle. Always have been. Spit it out. The truth. Why are you being mean to Bobby? Is it because of me?" His legs spread, his hands resting firmly on his hips.

"Not everything is about you, Calvin Morrison!" It was her turn to yell. Pent-up frustration bubbled inside her. She pushed away from him and strode into the living room, and he followed. Frustration at her condition, anger at having to reveal it to Cal, and pity for herself made a bad cocktail. She whirled on him.

"I can't help him because I *can't*! I can't see well enough to help him!"

"What?" He threw a confused look at her.

"That's right. I'm vision impaired. I have macular degeneration."

"I don't believe it," Cal said, shaking his head. "Only old people get that."

"Wrong! You don't believe me? Who the hell are you to say that to me?" she hollered.

He stood planted in the archway to the living room. "Your vision seems fine to me."

She grabbed his hand and dragged him into the kitchen. Picking up a mug, she splashed some water into it and swung it into the microwave. She set it for fifteen seconds.

"Fifteen seconds," the machine said.

Giselle pushed the stop button. "I have a talking microwave! Julia bought it for me. Who do you think spends a fortune for a talking microwave but someone who can't see the display or the buttons?"

Cal's mouth fell open. They stood, staring at each other. Despite her efforts, her eyes filled.

He finally found his tongue. He whispered, "Oh my God, Zell. That's terrible. I'm so sorry." The use of her former nickname broke her control.

She covered her face with her hands and sobbed. He scooped her into his embrace. Holding her close, he stroked her hair. "Oh, baby. When did this happen?"

Unable to stop crying, she melted into him, her face buried in his shoulder. Her tears soaked his shirt, but she didn't move. His hand traveled down her back. He held her to him, mumbling words she couldn't understand, except the word "baby," which he repeated again and again.

When she could control herself, she stepped back. A handkerchief rested in his hand. He offered it. She wiped her face and looked away.

"When did this happen?" he asked, his voice soft.

"It started three years ago."

"How much can you see?"

"It's my central vision that's going. I see light and shadows, shapes. Things are fuzzy. If it's magnified, I can see, even to read. But it needs to be huge."

"How do you deal?"

"I listen to audiobooks, have a talking microwave, use an electric stove, live on one floor because stairs aren't a good idea. I have peripheral vision. If I turn my head, I can see okay."

"I had no idea."

"I've organized my life, my house, so I can find things and get along. Of course, my design work is finished. I'm looking for something else. I'm considering dog-sitting, but having a dog around might be a problem. I might trip over him."

"I don't know what to say."

"What can you say? It sucks. But I've had three years to get adjusted, and I'm getting there."

"That's why you sold your house?"

"Yep."

"It's not going to get worse, is it? Will you become blind?" He placed his hands on her upper arms.

"The doctor said I'm stable, for now. But there are no guarantees. I'd never be totally blind, but I could lose all my central vision."

"And what would you see?"

"What you see, but with a big black circle in the middle."

Cal didn't let go. Giselle took advantage, snuggling into his shoulder. His body heat soothed her, like it used to. He kissed her hair.

"That's terrible. You're too young."

"But it's life. My life, anyway. So, I can't help Bobby, even if I wanted to."

"I'm sorry I yelled at you. I didn't know. Why didn't you tell me?" he asked, holding her away from him.

She gazed at the floor. "I didn't want you to know."

"I get that. Why?"

"I've had enough rejection because of it. And pity is worse. I know you'd do things, being helpful because you pity me. And I couldn't take that."

"Being helpful is bad?"

"Being helpful for the wrong reasons is." She raised her voice an octave. "Oh, look. It's poor, blind Giselle. We must help her, we must hold her arm when she takes the stairs." She cleared her throat. "Stuff like that would make me barf."

"I'd never do that."

"Really? Then you're different from most of the population." She turned away, wrapping her arms around her torso to ward off the chill settling in after she parted from Cal.

He put his hand on her shoulder. "Don't turn your back to me. We're talking."

"I'm done talking. You got what you came for. The truth."

"Does everyone in town know?"

"Only a few people."

"My mother?"

Giselle nodded, sensing heat in her face.

"You told her before me?"

"She wouldn't judge me."

When he drew in a big breath, she looked up. Staring hard didn't help, so she angled her head slightly to the right.

"You think I'd judge you because of this? Some physical thing you can't help?"

"Others have," she sniffed.

"Wow. Giselle. Really? You're judging me by the actions of strangers?"

"Maybe. When you put it that way, it sounds..."

"Ridiculous? It does." He moved toward the door. "I see you don't want me to bother you."

"I didn't mean that."

"Yes, you did."

She hung her head because he was correct. He knew her too well.

"I'm sorry." She reached out.

"So am I." He took her hand, squeezed it then opened the door.

When the lock clicked, she rested her forehead on the wall and cried.

Chapter Eight

Cal opened the door, relieved to see Bobby had dozed off watching the movie. He covered his son with a throw and turned off the tube then hit the kitchen and opened a beer. Though he'd been ordered not to drink alcohol, he needed something and figured beer was a whole lot better than whiskey.

He slumped down on a chair. Giselle's confession knocked the wind out of him. Holy hell. The impact of the enormity of her disability struck him like a bolt of lightning. He ran his hand over his face then shut his eyes. Pain in his heart grew. One by one, activities she couldn't do came to mind.

"Aha!" He sprang to his feet. "That's why she doesn't have a car!" Giselle would never drive again. Cal loved to drive, and the idea he'd never be able to drive again made his knees weak. The guy who picked her up...maybe he only drove her to the thrift shop and wasn't her boyfriend?

Could she watch television? Go to a movie? He had no idea. No wonder she dropped off audiobooks. Now, he understood why she and Bobby were listening to the Hardy Boys instead of reading.

He sipped his brew. Why wouldn't she tell him? Did she really believe he'd think less of her? Or treat her like some helpless invalid? Her response had cut him as surely as if she'd stuck a sword through his gut. Had he been a bad boyfriend? A callous lover?

He finished his beer and opened the refrigerator. Time to start dinner. He stopped. How does Giselle cook? He chuckled at the talking microwave. Bobby must love that. Was it safe for her to use a stove or build a fire?

He shook his head, his face heating with shame. That was exactly what she'd meant—people thinking she couldn't take care of herself. Giselle had always been smart. Surely, she knew what her limitations were and had figured out how to work around them.

He tossed a pound of ground meat in a skillet and chopped up an onion. As he prepared meat sauce for the spaghetti, he thought about his son. How could he tell him? Bobby would have a million questions Cal couldn't answer. He'd have to speak to Giselle. After his abrupt exit, it might not be easy to get her to even answer the phone.

For his boy's sake, he had to try. A wry grin spread across his face. To be honest, it wasn't only about his son. He didn't leave things with her in a good place, he'd been cold. Sure, she'd stabbed him, sort of, and he'd reacted. Pushing her away had been mean. She'd been honest with him, and he'd let his hurt feelings color his judgment, pulling away rather than tuning in on her pain and anguish. Damn. What the hell had he done? Or not done, in this case.

He reached into the fridge and grabbed another package of meat and a second onion. After adding everything to the pan, he picked up his phone. There was only one way to fix things, and that was head-on. *Don't be a coward. Man-up and get this done.*

"Giselle?"

"Yes?"

"Cal."

"Oh."

Then silence. He took a deep breath before speaking. "Can you come to dinner tonight? I'd like Bobby to know about...about your...uh, vision-thingy. I can't tell him because I don't know much. I'd appreciate it if you could tell him and answer his questions."

"Dinner?"

"Yeah. And answer mine, too."

"Bobby should hear it from me. I don't want him to think I simply wouldn't do the project."

"Good. I agree. Then you'll come?"

"Of course."

"I'm making spaghetti in meat sauce. You still eat meat?"

She laughed. "I do. You cook?"

"Yep. Not too bad, either. So I'm told."

"Fine. Great. Thank you for the invitation. What time?"

"Five thirty?"

"Fine. See you then."

She hung up. Damn! She'd agreed. He rubbed his face. Shit! He ran to the bathroom and peered at himself in the mirror. He looked like death warmed over and had a week's growth of beard. It might look good if it had been trimmed or tamed or something.

One whiff under his arm, and he started the shower. Stripping down, he face-palmed when he realized he'd had Giselle in his arms when he stunk like month-old cheese. Under the warm water, he scrubbed his body. Thoughts of Giselle joining him started blood pumping to his groin. No way could he mess with that.

He changed the water temperature to cooler and finished up. With a towel around his waist, he lathered up at the sink. Cal took all the scruff off and slapped a little aftershave on. He still used the same scent she'd picked out for him one Christmas.

He threw on a clean T-shirt and jeans and returned to the kitchen. Bobby sat at the table, rubbing his eyes.

"Hey, Buddy, go comb your hair, okay?"

"Why?"

"Gizelle's coming to dinner."

"She is?" Bobby leaped off his seat and ran to the bedroom.

Cal laughed. His son had one big-mother crush on Giselle Davenport. He smiled—guess both the Morrison men held a torch for the lady.

He rubbed his smooth face. The shower had revived him. His mother had picked out the new T-shirt, saying it was the color of his eyes. His hair needed a trim, too. But the turquoise of the garment did bring out the blue in his eyes. He might be shaggy, but a handsome man still stared back at him from the mirror.

Returning to the kitchen, he added the pasta to the boiling water. The doorbell rang. His stomach flipped. What the hell was wrong with him? This wasn't a date, was it?

BOBBY OPENED THE DOOR.

"Come in." He grabbed her sleeve and yanked her inside the house.

"Thank you." She sniffed the air. "Something smells good."

"Daddy's making pisgetti."

"Oh, I see." She nodded.

"Howdy," came from the living room. Damn, the timbre of his deep voice still made her shiver. "Come on in. Can I take your coat?"

"I'll do it." Bobby ripped the garment from her hands then ran to the hooks behind the door.

She smiled.

"You have two guys who want to help you here," Cal said.

"I see. Food smells great."

"Spaghetti is my specialty."

"I'm honored to be invited on such a special night," she said.

"Any night you're here is special," Bobby piped up.

"Glass of wine?" Cal asked.

"Sure."

"Red or white?"

"Red?"

"Perfect." Cal disappeared then returned with an open bottle and two glasses.

"Sit here. Next to me." Bobby climbed up on the sofa.

She followed his orders.

"We can do my project before dinner," he said.

"No time, Bobby. Giselle's not here to do your project."

"Why not?" Bobby yowled.

"She's gonna tell you why." Cal placed a glass of wine on the coffee table.

Giselle swallowed. She knew about where the glass was but feared reaching for it. She put her hand on the tabletop and slid it down to the glass then gently up the stem. The silence in the room caught her attention. With two hands, she brought the drink to her lips and took a small sip. Afraid to put it down, she held it, hoping it wouldn't spill. It had been a long time since she'd managed a wineglass.

"Would you rather have a smaller glass?" Cal asked.

She nodded. "Thank you."

"Why don't you like the glass, Giselle?" Bobby asked.

Cal took the stemware from her and left the room.

"I'm glad you asked." She took a deep breath, swallowed then began a stripped-down tale of her impaired vision. "A couple of years ago, something happened to me..."

The wiggly boy stopped moving and stared. At one point, he waved his hand in front of her eyes.

"Can you see my hand?"

"Yes. But if you stood across the room and waved at me, it would be a blur and I wouldn't know for sure it was your hand."

"When are you gonna get better?"

"I'm not, Bobby. This is the way it's going to be for me."

The boy burst into tears. "Everybody gets better."

She put up her hand as she felt a breeze. Cal rushed toward them. Before he could interfere, Giselle scooped the boy up and onto her lap. She hugged him tight. He clung to her.

"I want you to get better," he sobbed.

Tears clouded her eyes. "Thank you, Bobby, I know you do. Some-times, that doesn't happen. Will you still be my friend, even if I don't get better?"

The boy sniffled into a hanky his father gave him and nodded.

"All's good," Giselle said.

"I love you," Bobby mumbled.

Startled, Giselle eased him off her lap.

Settling into his seat on the sofa, the boy said, "I'm gonna marry you."

"What?"

The sofa dipped as Cal joined them. "Bobby, Giselle is your friend, but not your girlfriend. You're too young to get married."

"Will you wait for me to grow up?" the boy asked.

"Oh, Bobby. I love you, too, but not like that. Like a friend. Can't we be friends? Good friends?"

"Okay," he said, his voice soft and despairing.

"You understand why I can't help you with your project?" she asked.

He nodded.

"And you're not mad?"

He shook his head.

"I'm hungry." He pushed to his feet and headed to the dining room table.

"I'll be right there," Cal called to his son. He placed his hand on her forearm. "Are you okay?"

"Most heartfelt proposal I've ever received," she said.

Cal smiled. He took her hand and they joined his son at the dining table.

"Daddy, did you make bread?"

"Garlic bread? I sure did." He held out Giselle's chair then headed for the kitchen. Before long, he returned with a big bowl of steaming spaghetti, generously covered in meat sauce. A wooden bowl with salad stood to her left, next to a basket of garlic bread.

"May I serve you?" Cal picked up a large fork and spoon.

"Please." She handed him her plate.

They passed around a basket.

"I had no idea you had such talent in the kitchen." She savored the luscious food.

"Daddy makes good pisgetti," Bobby said, nodding.

Cal added, "You learn to develop skills when you have to."

"Oh yes. I'm sorry, I forgot."

As they ate, Bobby recounted his day at school. Cal spoke about the jobs he had lined up then explained the idea of the thrift shop to his son.

"When are you going to open it to the kids?" Cal asked.

"This week. I think tomorrow is the first day."

"Mrs. MacGregor said we have a surprise trip tomorrow."

"Maybe your school will be the first one to come through." Giselle tore a piece of bread in half.

"Are you ready?" Cal asked.

"As ready as I can be."

"I saw signs looking for volunteers. Anyone raise their hand?"

"Quite a few. Jory and Mindy have helped me set up. But more are coming tomorrow. I think your mom's on the list, too."

"Can you use one more?"

Her spine straightened. "I have enough, thank you."

"Gonna be like that, huh? Kind of stuck-up?"

Her lips compressed into a tight frown. "I told you."

"It's not pity. I only want to help."

Bobby put his fork down. Giselle sensed his gaze on her. She took a deep breath.

"Okay. Thank you."

"What time?"

"School kids are coming at nine. Each group for an hour."

"I'll be there early."

"The girls are coming early. Why don't you come at noon? I'll need help then."

"Okay. I'll be there."

She nodded. Damn it, she'd gotten along all this time without him. She didn't need him. They finished dinner. Giselle made up a bedtime story for Bobby, after Cal gave him a bath. She tucked Bobby in and kissed his forehead. Then came the hard part—saying good night to Cal.

She plucked her jacket off the hook and put it on. Cal held it for her. Her hands shook, making zipping it up hard. Cal moved in to help, but she turned away from him and zipped it up quickly.

"I don't need your help."

"Okay, sorry," he said, raising his hands.

"Thanks for dinner. And helping with Bobby."

"I always have his back."

She faced Cal. "I'd never hurt him."

He nodded and opened the door.

He closed his fingers around her biceps. "Wait."

Her heart thudded hard and fast, but she turned toward him. His mouth came down on hers. Try as hard as she might, she couldn't pretend she didn't want his kiss. Oh yes, she did. And more.

Starting sweet and gentle, it grew hungry in a flash. He pulled her against him as his tongue explored her mouth. Her eyes drifted shut, allowing her to focus on the desire sweeping through her. Her hands snaked over his shoulders, holding him fast.

With breathing coming quicker, she anticipated his touch. But it never came. Suddenly, he stepped back, allowing the cold air to chill her into reality.

"I'm sorry. Seems I still can't resist you."

She licked her lower lip, savoring the taste of Cal. She reached up to touch his cheek. "You shaved?"

He gazed down, his face coloring. "Yeah. I remembered you like it better that way."

She smiled and gave one nod. Oh, yes, she liked it better any way with Cal Morrison.

"Thanks again for dinner," she said, strolling toward the front step. Her hand instinctively reached for the short railing. Cal moved up beside her, like a spotter in gymnastics.

"See you tomorrow," he said, his breath warm on her ear, his deep voice vibrating in his chest so close to hers. Giselle stopped. Fear of rejection fought with longing.

"I have to go," she said as much to herself as to him.

"I know. Don't like it, but I understand."

She bolted. Grasping the railing with all her strength, she zipped down the stairs then across the lawn, fleeing while she had the strength.

AT TEN O'CLOCK, CAL stood by the window. The moon glowed big and bright in a cold, dark sky. He swirled the whiskey in his glass as he stared at Giselle's house. A thin shaft of light peeked out between her living room curtains.

Confused, hurting, and hating himself for not figuring out something was wrong with her before this, he frowned. It explained everything. Her tentative steps on the ice, falling, hanging on the railing at her front steps.

The way she held a glass or mug—with both hands and felt for the table before putting it down. The signs were all there, but he'd been too caught up in his hurt pride, pain that had simmered in his heart all these years, to see the truth. He'd let her down, and that hurt most of all.

Could they put their baggage from the past aside and try again? Could he have someone in his life, in Bobby's life, who was visually impaired? If they got together, could she be alone with his son? Would the boy be safe? He took a swig. Damn, he'd let Bobby go over there plenty of times and he'd been fine. How could Cal think she'd be any less capable now?

If it had been only the two of them, would he have cared? No, of course not. While he'd never expect it, her vulnerability made her even more attractive. Sure, she'd always been strong and independent. But now? Hell, he liked the idea she'd need him—if they lived together. And that was a big "if." It wasn't up to him alone, and he was far from sure they could put the past behind them. He'd have to deal with her leaving, and she'd have to make peace with his marriage—a couple of giant hurdles.

Did he want to try? He wasn't convinced it was possible, and the last thing he needed was a feud with the woman across the street. And then there was Bobby to consider. If they tried and failed, he'd get caught in the middle. Cal couldn't have that.

He rubbed the back of his neck. He needed answers, and a quick, honest guarantee she would love him again. But there was none. He'd have to take a chance with both his heart and Bobby's.

After Jane died, his mother had told him to get out there again, take a chance, meet someone. But he'd buried himself in work and his son. There had been no time to consider finding another woman. Giselle had still been abroad. He didn't want anyone else. And now that she'd returned, she was all he could think about.

He wanted guidance and thought about talking to his parents. But he knew what they would say. "Life without chances isn't living." It had been their mantra, regarding their only child. Cal couldn't disagree.

But he was older now, thirty-one, with a child to consider. He could hear his mother's words in his head, "How much happier would

Bobby be if you were happy?" His lips spread in a wry grin. She had a way of making the solution to any problem sound easy.

He finished his drink, washed out his glass, and put it in the drying rack. On the way to his bedroom, he checked in on Bobby. The boy was sound asleep. In his own room, Cal stripped down and got into bed. Tapping into his mother's point of view gave him positive energy. First step in this mess was to resolve things with Giselle. He needed to talk to her, alone, hash out old feelings, air old grievances. There was no way they could move forward, if that was in the cards, with that crap hanging between them.

First thing tomorrow, he'd make plans to have time with her. That was, after he helped at the thrift shop. Maybe that was the perfect time and place to talk. He laced his fingers behind his head and stared at the ceiling.

Two people had to agree to have that conversation. Was Giselle interested? His mind drifted back to their kiss. Damn, it was smokin'. When she put her arms around him, warmth traveled through him. He'd wanted her and could have taken her in a heartbeat if the circumstances had been different.

HE'D BEEN HER FIRST lover at the end of high school. Kids, fumbling around, not knowing what they were doing, still created heat. They'd had chemistry from their first conversation until their goodbye kiss at the bus station.

At his front door, Giselle had melted against him, boneless. He'd sensed a green light from her. Of course, he wouldn't have done anything without a definite go-ahead, but he figured she wanted him. Giselle Davenport was the same passionate woman he'd known years before.

The knowledge whetted his appetite. Simply thinking about her, the feel of her softness against him, her willingness, her lips, her scent tantalizing his nostrils made him hard. He recalled every sweet inch of her body. The attraction between them hadn't changed. Her beauty had grown over the years, not diminished.

He rolled over. Was he too old to have a wet dream? A man never grew too old for sexual release. He attempted to push sexy thoughts out of his head and fell asleep dreaming he was making love to Giselle in an empty field, like the good ole days.

Chapter Nine

At seven o'clock, Chris pulled up in the Bentley.

"Good morning. Ready for the big day?" he asked as he held the door open.

"I guess." Giselle climbed into the front seat.

After taking his place behind the wheel, he put the car in gear. "You sound a little nervous."

"Maybe. Not sure what I'll find there."

"I think you'll be pleasantly surprised."

"Why? What have you heard?" She faced him.

"Nothing, really."

"Come on, Chris. You're a bad liar."

"Okay, okay. I've heard everyone wants to help. I think you'll be happy with the number of adults who show up."

Giselle gave a tentative grin. "I hope you're right."

He pulled up in front of the thrift shop and opened her door. Offering his hand, he helped her out and escorted her to the door.

"You don't have to. I know the way."

"I want to."

She shrugged and curled her fingers around his biceps. On the way up the steps, she smelled something. The familiar aroma wafted to her nose. Once inside, a cry went up from a group of people. "Surprise!"

She could make out six people bustling about. Jory and Mindy came forward.

"What do I smell?" Giselle asked.

"Laura Dailey's cinnamon buns and gingerbread cookies," Jory said.

"The cookies are for the kids, but the cinnamon buns are for us!" Mindy added.

"Coffee's brewing in the back, too. Come on." Jory led the way.

Emotion choked Giselle. "I never expected..."

Jory hugged her friend. "I know."

"You did this without me knowing?"

"People want to help. They believe in what you're doing," Jory said.

The volunteers gathered around Giselle. Each had a cup of joe and a pastry. Giselle handed out tasks. There were six women, including Betty, Cal's mother. She pulled Giselle aside.

"Have you told him yet?" Betty asked.

"Cal?"

The older woman nodded.

"Yes. And Bobby, too."

"Oh good. How'd he take it?"

Giselle sighed and bowed her head. "Just the way you thought he would. He was shocked but very sweet and supportive."

"Thank God!" Betty let out a breath. "That's my son."

"I underestimated him."

Betty patted Giselle's shoulder. "No worries. It's hard to gauge how people will react. Let's get this going," Betty said then glanced at her watch. "The kids'll be here in an hour."

Bombarded with questions from her crew, Giselle hardly had time to catch her breath before a school bus pulled up to the curb. She straightened her flannel skirt and combed her short hair back with her fingers.

"Remember, every item is a quarter, unless the child has no money. Then it's free. Ready?" she asked.

A murmur of ascent met her ears. Her nerves kicked up. "Relax, Zell," she whispered to herself. "This part is supposed to be fun."

A middle-aged woman came through the door. "Hi, you Giselle Davenport? I'm Millie Fergus." The women shook hands. "And these are the first and second grade students from Pine Grove Elementary."

"Welcome," Giselle said. "Come on in and start shopping."

The children marched in, two by two, holding hands with their partner. Mrs. Fergus spoke up.

"Today, we're here to pick out presents for our families. It's not about you today, but about you having something to give to your mommy, daddy, brothers, and sisters for Christmas. Look at the shelves and tables. When you see something you want to give to a member of your family, raise your hand."

Giselle's ear caught strains of *Silver Bells*. Christmas music played in the background. Must be Jess, she was a fiend for every kind of song about the holiday. A tug on Giselle's skirt drew her attention.

"I want this," a little girl said.

The teacher bustled over. "That's fine, Melissa. I think your mom will love this sweater."

While Betty helped two little boys, Mindy and Jory manned a wrapping table. One by one, the children took their items over to be gift wrapped. Once they were done, they got a cookie and returned to the bus.

The remaining items got mussed up, out of order, and some ended up on the floor. After the first round of kids was loaded back on the bus, the women scurried around putting items back in place and bringing out a new batch of cookies.

Busload after busload came and went. Giselle heard the sounds of happy children and, even with her blurry sight, made out a few smiling faces in the crowds. Her heart warmed as she hustled up and down aisles, answering questions from the students and her volunteers.

THE LAST MORNING GROUP left at eleven forty-five, in time to return to school for lunch. Giselle blew out a breath and found a chair. She munched on a cookie as each of the women regaled the others with cute tales of the little shoppers.

"And when Kenny asked me if this razor was the only size we had, I almost lost it," Betty said.

Giselle sat back, listening. "I think this was the most inquisitive group we've ever had."

"Pretty damn choosy, if you ask me," Mindy piped up.

"Oh yes. They only want the best for their family," Jory agreed.

"Next group won't be here until one thirty. Might as well take a lunch break," Giselle said.

"Lunch? We've got a lot of straightening up to do," Betty said.

The tinkle of the bell over the door drew Giselle's eye. There weren't supposed to be any children for an hour and a half. The door creaked as it opened. The women were silent.

"Is this the place where a guy can find a good Christmas gift for his mom?" asked a deep, masculine voice.

"Cal?" Giselle stood.

"Don't get up. How's it going?"

The room was silent for a moment. Then, every one of the women mumbled some excuse and disappeared into the back room.

Giselle chuckled. "Seems like they think we want to be alone."

"Ya think?" Cal moved closer.

The scent of pine preceded him by a few seconds. *Damn, it's that sexy aftershave he wears.*

"Looks like you still got some stuff left," he said.

"You should see the back room. We've only begun to unload the donations."

"That's good. I expect you'll be cleaned out in the next couple of days."

"With any luck."

He took her hand between his two. A feeling of safety washed over her.

"I've been thinking. We need to talk. Clear the air."

"Talk?"

"Yeah. Talk about everything. Kinda get it sorted out. So we can move on."

She stiffened. "You want to move on?"

"Not like that."

"With me?"

"Sure as hell not with Santa Claus. Yes, with you. I'm not saying it right."

A wave of emotion engulfed her. Anticipation mixed with fear. Had the time come for a reckoning, an understanding? Would she get a chance to explain her side and finally find out why he got married? Did she want to know? Her heart leaped ahead several beats. She nodded.

"Good. After all this. Okay?"

"Okay," she coughed out.

"It's a date, then?"

"Yes."

"I'll get my parents to babysit."

"Good. Fine. If you promise to listen," she said.

"I will if you will." He folded his arms across his chest.

"Of course."

"Okay. I'll call you to set it up."

She nodded. At the sound of a throat clearing, Giselle looked up. Cal stepped away.

"I don't mean to interrupt, but we don't have much time before the next group," Betty said.

"Can I help? Put me to work," Cal said.

"Music to my ears! My son begging to work. Perfect. You can start by pulling down all the stuff on the top shelves in the storage room."

"Fine."

"Right this way," she said, leading Cal to the back.

Hmm, move on? Where would they be going? No time to ponder the ramifications now, Giselle had work to do, and a small staff to manage. She dusted the crumbs from lunch off her skirt and led the way.

"Let's get the books back on the shelves and fold the sweaters. Those should go fast." She picked up hardcovers and paperbacks from the floor. When Cal moved off, Giselle's pulse didn't slow down. Clear the air with Cal Morrison, could it be true? Would it happen? Could he forgive her? Could she forgive him?

Married, he'd gotten married and had a child—with someone else. How could she ever forget? He'd stomped on her heart and robbed her of her dream of marrying him and having his baby. Did she possess enough forgiveness in her heart?

Questions interrupted her concentration. Her thoughts scattered. Somehow, folding clothes and wrapping toys didn't seem as important as her ability to forgive the man she'd adored for forever. Did this mean she had a second chance with Cal? Or was it simply that he didn't like the bad blood between them, especially since they were neighbors.

She doubted it was so simple. He'd kissed her, hard, passionately. There was nothing "friendly neighbors" about his kiss. A shiver shot through her at the memory. Maybe Cal wanted her, in some way. Hell, she wanted him, she'd made it shamelessly obvious.

But forgive, too? Could she?

"Giselle? Are you present? With us?" Betty asked.

She sensed heat in her face. "Sorry, Betty. My mind was somewhere else."

"I think I can guess where," the older woman said, resting her hand on Giselle's arm.

"What? What do you need from me?"

"Nothing. I mean, where do you want these trucks?"

"In the blue bin. Red for cars, blue for trucks."

"Thanks," Betty replied then lowered her voice. "Please forgive him. He still loves you."

"Did he tell you to say that?"

"No. He'd kill me if he knew."

Giselle squeezed Betty's hand and prayed Cal's mother was right.

GISELLE FOUGHT TO STAY awake on the ride home.

"My scintillating personality putting you to sleep?"

"I'm sorry, Chris. I'm exhausted from a day filled with kids, clothes, toys, food, and friends. Wow. The energy was amazing."

"Did you give away a lot of stuff?"

"We did and we made ten dollars in quarters! Fortunately, we only have four more days. I think we'll have enough things for all the children. We did collect a huge amount of stuff."

"There were big bags out there every day for weeks."

"I didn't plan to do it this way. I figured we'd get a couple of bags of stuff and have kids in for half a day. But it got way out of control."

"Is that a bad thing?"

"My mom would be so happy to see how this thing has taken off."

"She started it?"

"After I was in middle school. It took a couple of years to organize and get going. But now it's a damn monster!" she said, laughing.

"It's something to be proud of."

"Recycling in the best way."

Chris dropped her and waited for her to get inside before he pulled away. Giselle stopped at the liquor cabinet. She poured a glass of her father's favorite sherry and headed for the sofa. She took a few hefty swigs, lay down, and pulled the throw over her. Too tired to start the fire, she closed her eyes.

Visions of Cal popped into her mind. What did he really want? And what did she want? Now that her design work had ended, she had no career. One couldn't make the thrift shop full-time work. Once the holidays were over, she'd go back to keeping it open two days a week and charging more than a quarter for merchandise. But such paltry income would barely pay the heating bill.

While her body needed rest, her mind refused to close up shop. She needed to earn a living or her financial reserves would disappear quickly. What could she do? Not much. Maybe something involving the school?

Finally, her body took over and Giselle conked out. In the morning, she arose late and raced around getting a fast shower, dressing quickly, and gulping down one cup of coffee. Chris was right on time.

The sun had melted the ice on her path and warmed the air to an acceptable thirty degrees. She strode toward the street, waving at Chris. After sliding into the front seat, she smiled. Day two of Santa's Thrift Shop, and she was ready.

When she arrived at eight thirty, warm cookies were on plates, scones were in baskets, and the smell of brewing coffee blended with the aroma of butter and sugar.

"Where did we get a coffeemaker?" she asked Jory.

"Someone donated it, so we decided to use it. You can give it away on the last day."

"Give it away? No way. We've always needed a coffeemaker. We can sell cups of coffee for fifty cents or give them away to customers. Maybe it would help sales?"

"Now you're thinking like a businesswoman," Mindy said.

"Me? A businesswoman?" Giselle laughed.

"Yes. This idea is spectacular. Suppose thrift shops all across the country started doing this? Think of the goodwill generated. Think of how you'd be bringing true giving back to Christmas."

"I hadn't thought of that."

"You should. We'll talk after Christmas. I have a few ideas I'd like to share with you," Mindy said.

"Great."

At nine fifteen, the first busload of kids pulled up to the curb. Fifteen children filed into the store, and the place jumped to life. Cookies disappeared into little hands while clothing, books, gadgets, and small appliances were wrapped as gifts. Candy dishes, vases, brooches, necklaces, and scarves were covered in pretty paper, ready to be nestled under a Christmas tree.

At twelve, they took a one-hour lunch break. Giselle sat for the first time that day, happy to rest. Boisterous, enthusiastic, and discerning shoppers, the children asked a million questions and seemed to touch every item in the shop. Once again, tidying up was on the agenda before the next group of students arrived.

Giselle opened the bag containing her lunch and took a bite of her sandwich.

"I can't believe how many kids we have this year," Jory remarked.

"I know," said Laura Dailey. "Word has traveled."

"How far did Barney go with those posters? I wouldn't be surprised to see a group from Timbuktu," Giselle teased.

"He did get a bit carried away. I'm guessing we'll have a couple of groups from Willow Falls," Laura put in.

"That's pretty far. But it's okay with me," Giselle said.

At three thirty, after the last group left, Cal showed up. "Thought you might need some help straightening up. Hope you don't mind that Bobby wanted to come."

"Not at all. Bobby, can you gather the cars and trucks and put them in the bins?"

"Sure," he said, getting right to the task.

"Put up a full pot," Betty called to Laura. "Cal's here."

"Free coffee? This place is gettin' classy," he said.

"We're keeping the coffeemaker," Giselle said.

"You can call off your ride. I'll take you home," Cal said.

Giselle called Chris and cancelled. When they finished, Cal offered his arm as they descended the stone steps to his truck. Bobby squeezed between them for the short ride home.

"There's Mikey. Can I go play, Dad?"

"Sure."

The boy climbed over Giselle and ran across the lawn to meet his friend. Cal turned to her.

"How about Saturday night?"

"What?"

"Saturday. Night. For our, uh, talk?"

"Oh. Yeah. Sure."

"You free?"

"I'm free every night." She chuckled.

"Good. Can I take you to dinner?"

"We can't talk in a restaurant. I can make dinner."

"Don't bother. I can pick something up."

"It's no trouble. I don't mind."

"Okay, then. What time?"

"Seven?"

"Works for me."

"See you then."

Cal helped her out of the truck. Inside, Giselle lit a fire and heated up leftovers. As she ate, she thought about what Mindy had said. Could she make something out of the Santa's Thrift Shop idea? And what about Cal? What would she say to him?

One more day of student shoppers and she'd be facing both those challenges. Excitement mixed with curiosity and fear—a powerful concoction.

CAL MADE DINNER, GAVE Bobby a bath, and put him to bed early. The boy was tuckered out from such a busy day, and his father needed the quiet time to think. He poured a whiskey on the rocks and sat in the living room, staring at the sky and Giselle's house. Wisps of smoke rose from her chimney, and the lights were dim.

Cal worried about the approaching date with her. Where would he begin? Should he apologize? Really? For doing what they had agreed to? Maybe for being irresponsible and not using a condom with Jane.

He couldn't help but wonder how different life would be if he had. Giselle might have returned a whole lot sooner and they'd have married. Anger at himself flushed through his chest. How stupid not to use a condom! But he hadn't planned on having sex. Two bottles of wine, a lonely, horny existence, and a willing woman seduced him into throwing caution to the wind.

And he'd paid the price. Did his foolish move make Giselle pay for his mistake, too? Maybe. Of course, if she hadn't taken off to Europe, they definitely would have married and none of this would have happened. He hadn't proposed to her, though. But he'd figured she'd have said yes. Cal pushed to his feet and headed for his bedroom.

He opened the top drawer and plucked out a small, velvet box. Upon returning to the sofa and downing another swig of his drink, he opened it. The diamond was small—all he could afford at the time. But the ring was delicate and beautiful, like Giselle.

He'd kept it all these years. Why hadn't he given it to Jane? Because he'd bought it for Giselle, and there was something grubby about giving it to another woman. They hadn't had time for an engagement ring. It was city hall fast and a plain gold band.

Through the years, Cal would pick up the box from time to time and stare at the ring. And he'd kick himself for not selling it. No reason to keep it. Still, it rested in his drawer, as a reminder. Giselle was a million miles away, and he hadn't even spoken to her for years. He wouldn't be placing it on her finger.

But now, he wasn't so sure. Restless, he wandered from room to room, staring out the window at the moon, looking for guidance. He didn't dare call his parents. He knew what they'd say—fall on your knees, beg forgiveness, and propose marriage. They both loved Giselle and were surprised when he married Jane. Hell, he was surprised when he married Jane.

But they adored Bobby and mourned with him when Jane died. He needed to find out what Giselle had been up to those years in Europe. Especially the months before he got married. Had she found someone else? She'd never told him who she'd dated or slept with. Giselle was a beautiful, desirable woman. He couldn't imagine her living like a monk.

As painful as it might be, he needed to know her history. How soon after she left him had she started dating and sleeping with other men? How many were there? Had she ever thought of him? Was she upset when she found out he was married...or relieved? Had she planned to marry anyone else? So many questions swirled through his mind.

He'd have to wait until Saturday to get answers. He hoped he'd get the truth. It would give him time to figure out what to ask. He needed to be ready and not fumfering around like some idiot. No more fumbling for words. Think it out, know what to say, and simply say it, damn it! Like a man, not a little schoolboy, shy in front of the teacher.

Cal knew the kind of life he wanted. He had two-thirds of it, and it was time to get the last piece. If Giselle wouldn't or couldn't be part of his life, then he'd better find out now and move on. He'd try online dating if he had to. Cal had lived too long without a woman. He needed a wife, and Bobby needed a mother. And the waiting and excuses were over.

This would be it for Giselle and Cal—do-or-die time. Fish or cut bait. She had to make up her mind—they both had to decide to forgive each other and start fresh. Could he do that? He thought so. Could she? A shiver of doubt shot up his spine. She'd have a lot to forgive and put behind her. He had no idea if she could do that or even wanted to. Saturday, he'd have the answer, good or bad. His mouth felt dry. He swallowed. Facing the facts might be harder than he'd imagined.

"Can I face the truth? I can if she can," he said to himself then chugged the last of the whiskey in his glass.

Chapter Ten

Saturday morning, the day of the date with Cal, Giselle awoke nervous. She planned to make beef stew. All men love stew, right? Rising from bed at six after tossing for an hour, she shoved her arms in a robe and schlepped to the kitchen.

Almost by rote, she filled the coffeemaker and turned it on. After hitting the "on" button on the radio, she yawned and took a seat, awaiting the brew. Christmas music played. It was only a week away now. She'd pushed thoughts of the holiday out of her mind because she'd be spending it alone.

Her aunt Julia had a date to celebrate with her Manhattan boyfriend. Giselle would be on her own. She'd ordered special food and a few new audiobooks from the library. Still, it sucked to be alone at Christmas. Aunt Julia had left a present on the windowsill for Giselle, and she'd given one in return.

Her smile faded when she thought of how she'd helped so many children find gifts for their families at the thrift shop, and she had taken none. As her mother had taught her, she'd purchased a few small items to have in the house should she feel the need to repay someone or return a kindness with a gift. Then there was the present for Bobby. She'd given that to Cal to put under the tree on Christmas Eve.

He'd done it willingly, with a small smile, instead of the grumpy response she'd expected. It couldn't be that Cal allowed her a small place in his son's life, could it? She'd settle for a little victory.

Sending gifts to her friends in Europe proved to be too costly, so she'd settled for sending cards. Her aunt had signed and addressed them for her. There was no way around it, Giselle had the pre-Christmas blues.

Once she had her first sip of coffee, she set about gathering the ingredients for her stew and tossing them in the Crock-Pot. She had the kind that turned on either high or low with no other settings, making it easy for her to do it right. She flipped it on low and got a fire started before she took a bath. By the time Cal arrived, a nice blaze would have warmed the room.

A long soak in the tub would be just the thing. The lily of the valley fragranced bath oil soothed her. She entered the water slowly, letting the heat sink into her bones, relaxing her.

After washing up, she lay there, thinking. What would she say to Cal tonight? She had no clue. Her mind centered on the questions he had for her. Her lips compressed into a frown as she formulated one theory after another about his marriage. What the hell was that about, anyway?

Lying there, Julia's words, when she learned of the date, came back to her.

"What do you want to accomplish with this meeting?" she had asked.

"To clear the air," Giselle answered out loud. "No. To get the facts? Maybe. To stop being angry and jealous that he got married? Yeah."

"Can you forget about his marriage?" Julia had continued.

"I don't know. Forgive? Maybe. After I have the facts. Maybe."

"And if you can't forgive, why are you wasting time with him? How can anything go forward if you can't get past the marriage?"

"Good question, Julia. I never thought he'd hurt me. It seemed intentional."

"Get the facts, Giselle, before you draw conclusions," Julia had advised during that conversation.

"I will. I will."

"Do you love him?" had been Julia's big question.

"I don't know. Maybe. Well, yes, probably. Maybe. No, I do. Yes." Giselle's thoughts turned to his kind acts, his protective attitude, his amazing parenting, and his handsome face. How could she not love him? Was he perfect? No. But maybe right for her.

When her fingertips shriveled, Giselle got out of the tub. She put on leggings and a flannel shirt. No bra? The baggy shirt covered well enough she didn't need one. Yawning, she crawled into bed and zonked out.

Two hours later, she awoke. Refreshed, she tackled straightening up her living room, cleaning up the kitchen, setting the table, checking the stew, and defrosting some frozen cream puffs for dessert. Those had been Cal's favorites.

She uncorked a bottle of merlot and cracked the windows to get fresh air. When she hit the button on her clock, it recited the time.

"It's five forty-five."

Time to put on makeup then stretch out on the sofa and listen to her new book. Before she'd listened to more than two chapters, the doorbell rang. Giselle jumped up, knocking her iPad to the floor. Scrambling to turn off the book, stow the iPad, comb her hair with her fingers, she called out, "Coming! Just a minute."

She grabbed a lipstick from the pocket of her shirt and swiped it on with seasoned efficiency and padded, barefoot, to the door. After taking two deep breaths, she mumbled softly, "Calm down. Calm down. He's not God."

She straightened her shirt, and reached for the doorknob.

"GRANDMA SAID I COULD make a gingerbread house," Bobby said.

Steering his truck along the streets of Pine Grove, Cal grinned. "Did she now?"

"Yep. She said we might have some cookies left for you, too."

"Oh yeah?"

"Yeah. She said, if you're good, you get cookies."

Cal laughed. "That's Grandma."

He pulled into his parent's driveway and put the car in Park. Before he turned off the engine, he faced his son. "Now, what are the rules?"

"Listen to Grandma and Grandpa and do what they say."

"And, what else?"

"Say 'please' and 'thank you.'"

"And?"

"That's all."

"Nope. One more."

Bobby's brow wrinkled. "Oh, I know! Eat what's on my plate."

"Right!" Cal ruffled his son's hair and hugged him. Bobby squealed in delight. "Come on, buddy. Let's go." Cal grabbed the backpack and exited the vehicle.

Cal and Bobby trekked through snow, taking a shortcut to the porch. His father opened the front door, and his mother pulled her grandson into a big hug.

"I'm so glad you're here," she said.

The aroma of gingerbread was unmistakable.

"That smells so good, I might have to stay," Cal joked.

"No, you don't, buster," his mother said, frowning. "Give me his bag and be on your way."

"Yeah, Dad. Be on your way," Bobby echoed.

Cal and his father cracked up. Betty helped the boy off with his jacket and boots then shepherded him into the kitchen.

"Coffee, Cal?" his father asked.

Cal checked his watch. "No time, Dad. But thanks."

Bobby raced to the door. He threw himself at his father, hugging his legs. Cal knelt down, pulling the boy into his embrace. A small stab of pain flew through him, as it always did when he left his son for the night.

"You'll be all alone, Dad. Why don't you stay here and make a gingerbread house?"

Cal straightened, sensing a flush in his face. "I'll be fine, Bobby." If he told his son the truth, that he was having dinner with Giselle, he would want to join them.

"We want to have some special time with you, Bobby," Betty said.

"I'm sure Cal will find something to do," his father said, a lecherous gleam in his eye.

The look from his dad ratcheted up the heat in Cal's face. Time for him to hit the road.

"Be good, son," Cal said then made tracks to the truck.

He heaved a sigh of relief to be pulling out of the driveway. Damn, was his father a dirty old man or what? He laughed. Guess he was young once, too. Cal put the truck in the garage and headed for the bathroom.

He took an extra-long shower. Out of habit, he wrapped a towel around his waist and lathered up his face. He needed to be smooth. Padding into the living room, he put on a best of Dolly Parton album. As he shaved, he listened. When the song, "Here You Come Again" came on, he stopped to sing along and even dance a few steps to the catchy tune.

The song summed up Giselle Davenport. Damn, just laying eyes on her got his blood pumping. A couple of the guys on the high school football team called her a "wet dream on legs" behind her back. He resented their remarks, feeling it a slur, but he knew they were right. But not only because her curves were perfect and the jiggle in her breasts and butt tempted him to touch her, but because she was the nicest person, outside of his parents, he'd ever met.

When he got banged up during a game, she'd hung back to make sure he got a ride home. He'd limped off the field and been too injured to drive. She hadn't even known him then. It was their first meeting. Coach knew her father, who'd been a big football booster, and made the introduction. She'd let Cal into her car with no worry about his behavior. Of course, he'd been a perfect gentleman. But that was Giselle—always helping others. He was half in love with her by the time he got home.

And now he had another chance. An opportunity to get it right.

"How many guys get it?" he asked his image in the mirror. "Not many. Don't fucking blow it this time."

He combed his hair ten, twelve, fifteen times to make sure every hair was where he wanted it. Then he stood in front of his open closet door, rubbing his chin and perusing the poor excuse for a wardrobe facing him.

"How come I don't have any decent clothes?"

Maybe because he hadn't been on a date since his wife passed, three years ago. Frowning, he pawed through every pair of jeans and every T-shirt. Nope, the T-shirts wouldn't cut it. When he got to the back of his closet, he found a shirt his mother had given him two Christmases ago, or was it three. A flannel shirt, kind of a turquoise-and-beige plaid. Damn, it was brand new! He'd struck the mother lode. Now to find jeans.

All his jeans had been pressed into service for work and were a mess, stained with pine sap, ripped—but not in a good way—or simply faded and worn.

"Gotta get some new jeans," he said, shaking his head.

He pulled on boxers then it came to him. *Damn! Mom bought pants that year, too. She said I needed one date-night outfit.* He rummaged through the back of his closet again until he came across a pair of khakis. Perfect! The flannel shirt and the good pants, damn, they still had a crease, would make this a real date. And he'd look good. Maybe she wouldn't be able to resist him.

"Thanks, Mom. I owe you one," he said to the mirror.

After shrugging the shirt over his broad shoulders, he buttoned it up, threaded a worn belt through the loops on the pants, and stepped into them. Closing the bedroom door, he checked his image in the full-length mirror.

"I look good," he said, nodding and smiling. "Not bad for a lumberjack."

He fished a clean pair of socks with no holes in them out of the bottom drawer and slipped them on. Shoes didn't matter. He'd wear his boots and take them off at her place anyway. Gee, would he be taking anything else off? He snickered as he headed for his dresser. Yep, he still had half a box of condoms. Feeling optimistic, he shoved two in his wallet and headed for the living room.

Oops! Damn. Forgot the aftershave. He took a detour through the bathroom and slapped on his favorite spicy scent, "Woodsy Guy", and checked his watch. Ten of, perfect timing. He slid his feet into his boots, grabbed his jacket, the bouquet of pink roses he'd set on the front hall table, and, nerves dancing, made his way across the street.

"CAL?" GISELLE ASKED, standing in the doorway.

"These are for you." He thrust the flowers at her.

"They're beautiful." She took the bunch, but her gaze took him in from head to toe.

"Can I come in?" he asked.

"Oh, of course, of course. Sorry." She stepped aside while she buried her face in the blooms. "It's just that you look so different."

"You mean 'cause I'm dressed like a human being instead of a lumberjack."

"Uh, yeah. That could be it." She chuckled then shut the door.

"Something smells good. Besides you, I mean."

Could he be nervous? Really? With me? She smiled. "I made stew. I hope you like it."

"I love stew."

She headed for the kitchen, and he followed. "I think there's a vase or a big pitcher on the top shelf," she said, opening a cabinet. "Could you get it down for me, please?"

"Sure." He reached up, grabbed the square vase, and set it on the counter.

"Want a drink? Beer? Wine? Whiskey?"

"What are you having?"

"I dipped into the merlot already. But you can have whatever you want." She felt in a drawer and plucked out a large pair of scissors. *Aren't we polite. It's like a first date.*

She cut a few inches off the bottom of the stems then arranged the flowers in the vase. "They smell so nice and look so pretty. Let's see, where should they go? I know..." She placed the vase on the dining table.

"That's perfect," he said.

Cal stood close behind her. She could smell him. Goose bumps rose on her arms. She rubbed them away then turned, placing her hands on his shoulders. On tiptoe, she kissed his cheek.

"Thank you. I love flowers."

"I remember," he said, slipping his arm around her waist, preventing her from leaving. Easing her closer, he lowered his mouth to hers. He tasted good, and his warm, soft lips coaxed her to open. She did, and his tongue danced with hers. Her fingers gripped his shoulders. She enjoyed the softness of his flannel shirt against her fingertips. His chest pressed against hers, raising heat in her. Before she lost control, Giselle eased back from him.

"We'd better eat. Don't want the stew to be overcooked."

"Oh, stew. Yeah. Sure." But he ran his thumb down her cheek before stepping back and letting her lead the way.

She'd set places ahead of his arrival. Cal carried wineglasses and the bottle to the table, where he filled them—a small glass for her, normal one for him. Then he toted the heavy stew pot and set it down next to her.

"Would you do the honors?" she asked, offering him the ladle. Did he know she wasn't comfortable maneuvering it with him watching? Probably. Cal was no fool.

They ate in silence for a few minutes.

"This is amazing." He speared a piece of meat.

"Thank you."

"The salad!" Giselle jumped up and rushed into the kitchen. She retrieved the glass salad bowl from the fridge and brought it back.

"Looks great." Cal took the bowl from her hands and set it down.

"I can't believe I almost forgot it. I'm so nervous. You'd think this was our first date," she said.

"You feel it, too? I thought it was just me."

"You, too?" She laughed. "We're like a couple of teenagers."

"Only we're not," he said, his voice quiet.

"Let's finish eating before we get into the, ah, talk, discussion, whatever. Okay?"

He nodded.

Giselle barely tasted the food. Her mind went over what she wanted to say, questions to ask, explanations to offer.

When they finished, Cal cleared the dishes away and refilled their glasses.

"Dessert?" she asked.

"I'm too full. Let's get to it. Waiting is just making it worse."

"Worse?" She frowned.

"You know what I mean."

"Not sure I do. It's been a while."

"People don't change," he said.

"They do, sometimes. If something like a hardship happens. If they lose a job or go broke or get sick."

"I s'pose. But inside, they're still the same."

Giselle pushed up from the table and strolled into the living room, drink in hand. "Let's get comfortable."

Cal followed. They sat facing each other on the long sofa. "Ladies first."

Giselle's nerves kicked up. She took a deep breath then swallowed. A swig of wine dampened her dry mouth. "Where should I start?"

"How about with your decision to go away?"

"Oh. I thought I'd told you about that?"

"I don't think so. All I remember hearing is that you were taking a job in Europe and would be back. In a year, maybe."

"After I got my degree, my professor told me about a job, working for a firm in Paris, designing office space. He said they were looking for an apprentice, but the job would be real, and, in three months, if I was good enough, I'd get promoted."

"Okay," Cal said. "And then?"

"The job was only for a year. They had a couple of projects they needed help with."

"And after a year?"

"I would come home. My mother thought it was the opportunity of a lifetime. She said I shouldn't pass it up." Giselle took another breath and more wine. "She said you'd still be here after a year." She stopped, bowed her head, and gripped her glass. "But she forgot to say that you might be married."

"I know what you said. But I didn't believe it. No way would you come back to Pine Grove after living in Paris. Who gives up Paris, Rome, London, for a tiny hick town? To me, you were gone for good."

"When I left, I'd already bought my return ticket. I was coming back."

"I didn't hear from you. Emails stopped coming."

"I got busy. If you're in Europe for your once-in-a-lifetime experience, you don't sit around moping about your boyfriend being home.

You see and do everything you can while you're there." She cleared her throat. "You trust he's home, being faithful."

"I was. Until you slowed down your emails. Then they stopped. By the way, you never told me you'd already bought a return ticket."

"Didn't do me much good. When I found out you were married, I canceled my flight."

He shifted in his seat.

She looked up at him, tears in her eyes. "I cried for weeks. Months. When they found out I didn't need to return to the States, the firm asked me to stay. And I accepted. No reason to rush home, was there?" As much as she tried to keep bitterness out of her voice, she didn't succeed.

CAL GAZED AT THE FLOOR, avoiding her eyes. Giselle snapped out in a tight voice, "What happened?"

Cal pushed to his feet, walked to the window, stared for a moment then returned. "It's complicated. I don't really remember who first said we should see other people."

"You said it was me, but I doubt it. If my memory's right, it was you."

He hung his head. No sense in trying to wiggle out of that one. She had him. "Okay. Yeah. It was me. Dumbest thing I ever said. I waited for you to object." He looked straight at her. "But you didn't."

She glanced at the floor. "Maybe I should have. Made a fuss or something. No, I didn't. So maybe that's on both of us."

"Young and stupid." He shook his head. "We'll figure it was a mutually agreed thing. I was mad. Damn mad. You were leaving. I had plans."

"Plans?"

"Yeah. Marriage plans. For you and me."

"You neglected to tell me," she said.

"Look, please, let me finish before you tear my head off."

"Okay."

"I was pissed, real pissed. The day you left I got drunk. I was up all night, puking."

She hugged a pillow to her chest.

"Honest. I wanted to turn you over my knee and give you the spanking of a lifetime."

"Spanking? I wasn't a child!" She rose to her feet.

"Sit down, sit down. You gonna let me finish?"

"Yes." She sank back down onto the sofa.

"I was mad. After the first two months, I got tired of being alone. Watching TV. So, I went to Homer's. Just to have a drink." He stopped to take a breath. Giselle cocked an eyebrow at him. "Okay, I went a couple of times. Maybe three or four times a week. Homer gave me a couple of free beers, and I met friends there. Then, one day, Jane walked in."

"The love of your life, I suppose?" Giselle's tone was frosty.

"Please, just listen."

She made a face, sipped her wine, and said, "Continue."

"She flirted with me, and so I took her out. We dated a couple of times. Nothing hot and heavy. She was nice, pretty. I liked her. She wasn't you, but, hell, you'd agreed I could date other women, so I did, occasionally. Now listen real careful to this part," he said, moving closer to her. "I had no intention—are you listening?—no intention of falling in love with anyone. Or even sleeping with anyone. Dating was a way to pass the time. That's it!" He stopped to take a drink.

"Really? So, what happened between, 'no intention of falling in love' and 'I do'?"

"Snarky. You've always been snarky. Some things never change," he said, casting her a dark glance. "She invited me over to her place for dinner. We finished off two bottles of wine. One thing led to another, and we spent the night together."

Giselle cringed. She bowed her head, but he saw a tear escape before she wiped it off her cheek. She sat doubled over and silent. Though she didn't speak, her pain spoke for itself. His gut tightened.

"I'm sorry, Giselle. You said you wanted the truth." He paused. "Say something."

She shook her head. If she'd punched him in the face, it would have felt better than her silence.

"I didn't plan it. It just happened. And speaking of not planning. Yes. We had unprotected sex. I didn't mean to. I never did it before. You and I always used condoms. But this time, one time we were drunk, horny, lonely, and it just happened. There. Is that what you wanted to hear?" He sighed.

"Go on," she croaked.

"You know the rest. A few weeks later, Jane told me she was pregnant and was keeping it. We went to city hall and got married. What else could I do? She was carrying my child, I had to step up."

Giselle spoke. "If you're waiting for me to say I'm proud of you for doing the right thing, I can't. I just can't."

"Do you disagree?"

"No. But you never told me. My mother did."

"What could I say? 'Hi, Giselle, by the way, I knocked up another girl and got married. How's your day been?' Really?"

She took another swig of wine and paused. "I suppose."

He grabbed her forearms. "I went through hell. Do you think I loved her? No. Do you think I wanted to marry her? No. Don't think for one second I didn't hate myself. I was a traitor, and I was going to pay—chained to a woman I didn't love and lose out on the one I did. It was all about Bobby. I did it for him."

Giselle raised wet eyes to his. "I didn't know. I thought you didn't love me anymore. Thought you loved her, instead. That you never loved me. I thought you'd forgotten me in five minutes, met someone else, and liked her better. I was discarded. Forgotten. Gone five months, and it was like we had never happened."

She covered her face with her hands, sobbing.

"It wasn't anything like that," he said, his voice softening. "I never stopped loving you."

He took her in his arms and stroked her hair. God it felt good to have her close to him, to be holding her. He closed his eyes and inhaled her sweet scent and lily of the valley perfume.

"Oh God, Cal. I was so brokenhearted. I couldn't eat. I lost fifteen pounds. Then I hated you for your treachery. For your duplicity."

"You hated me?" He let her go.

"Of course. But a year later, when I heard about Bobby, I had an inkling that it might have been a shotgun marriage."

"And?"

"And I stopped hating you. But I never stopped being sad. I never stopped regretting my decision to take the job."

"You did?"

"Oh yes. When I heard you got married, I realized if I'd stayed, that probably would have been me marrying you."

"And did you want to?"

She plucked a tissue from a box and mopped her eyes. "More than anything," she whispered. He drew her into his arms for a powerful hug.

"What about you?" He moved back.

"Huh?" She shot him a quizzical glance.

"Weren't you dating, too?"

"In the beginning, there was so much to learn about the job, I had no time for anything but work and an occasional glass of wine with a colleague. But after I heard about your marriage, I allowed some of my new friends to fix me up."

He stiffened. "Were you sleeping with anyone?"

She shifted in her seat.

Chapter Eleven

She sensed her face heating. "Not at first. Not for a long time."

"Really?" He cocked an eyebrow.

"Honest. I didn't. I didn't want to sleep with anyone but you. And if I couldn't have you, I only wanted friendships."

"But that changed?"

"When I found out you were married, all bets were off."

"Aha! So, there was someone. You were sleeping with someone?"

"To be honest, there were several men. But Gunther was the most serious."

"Gunther?"

"A handsome German who was on assignment in Paris. He flattered me. I dated him."

"Slept with him?"

"Slept with him for about six months."

"And?" Cal coaxed, narrowing his eyes.

"And he proposed."

"He proposed?" Cal's eyebrows shot up. "Really? You were engaged? How come I never knew about that?"

"I don't know. Maybe because it didn't last long."

"What happened?"

"That's about the time I found out about the macular degeneration. After I told Gunther, he dumped me. It was over fast."

"Oh my God. Really? No wonder you were reluctant to tell me."

"I didn't tell you because I didn't want your pity. I couldn't stand it."

"I'm sorry you have to deal with this, but you seem to be handling it well. He really walked out on you? What an asshole." Cal shook his head.

She nodded. "I was furious. But deep down, I knew I didn't love him like I loved you."

"Did or do?"

She faced him, silently.

"You're not going to answer? I thought this was a night of truth," he said.

"About the past."

"I see. So, you got dumped. And my wife was arrogant and foolish and died as a result. Now we're alone. Free. What are we going to do about it?"

"What do you want to do about it?" Fear coiled in her stomach.

"Okay, you're too scared to speak, so I will. I want you back. That's what I want to do about it. I want to be with you." He sounded confident, but his hand trembled when he picked up his wineglass.

"You do? Even with this?" She gestured toward her eyes.

"I do. I don't care about that. We'll deal with it. You're still you. What about you?"

"Oh, Cal. That's what I want, too."

And before she could speak again, he'd drawn her into his arms and kissed her. The rush of emotions almost knocked her over. Closing her mind, she opened her heart and wound her arms around his neck. Cal was back. Her Cal. And he wanted her, even with her disability.

Cal pushed to his feet, taking her with him. They stood, locked in a kiss. His fingers slid from her waist to her hips. He moved his fingers down to her bottom, which he squeezed. A groan escaped his throat as she came up flush against him.

Emotion welled up inside, mixing with desire. God she wanted him in every way. He slipped his hand underneath her flannel shirt and moved it up to cover her breast. As soon as his thumb made contact with her nipple, she jumped.

"Is that okay?" he whispered.

"Yes, yes, don't stop," she breathed.

The low chuckle emanating from him brought a smile to her lips.

"Come on," he said, leading her to the bedroom.

Padding along behind Cal, Giselle's body came alive, as if someone had shoved her big toe in a light socket. From behind, she watched his strong shoulders, begging her to touch him. As she walked, she unfastened the top button on her shirt. *Let's not waste time.*

Once inside her room, he stopped short and spun around, facing her.

"I want you," he said, his voice husky.

"Me, too," she replied.

He crushed her against him, his mouth attacking her with hungry kisses. Pushing up on tiptoe, she clasped her arms behind his neck. Once again, his palms landed on her rump. She lifted a leg and swung her foot around behind him. He picked up on it and cradled her thigh in his big hand before squeezing it. He ran his fingers up, lightly brushing her sex through her leggings. His touch ignited a fire in her that couldn't wait.

She pushed away from him and attacked his shirt, practically ripping the buttons off. He caught the fever and did the same to her. Once the shirts were open, he shrugged his to the floor and she tossed hers on a chair.

Cal ripped his T-shirt over his head and let it fall. Giselle stood half-naked in front of him.

"Holy hell. They're still great," he muttered, approaching her, his hands open and on her breasts in a heartbeat.

Her eyes closed for a second, enjoying the feel of his touch. Then she stared at his chest for a moment before running her fingers through his chest hair.

"You work out?"

"Yeah. Damn, Giselle. Damn." He bent to kiss her flesh.

Her fingers fumbled with his belt. Once it was open, he pulled the snap and unzipped the fly. She pushed his pants down then his boxers. The man stood stark naked and hard as stone before her.

"Now you," he said, hooking his thumbs in either side of her leggings and sliding them down. She stepped out of them, and they joined her shirt on the chair. He moved back. She sensed his stare, warming her.

"You are still the most beautiful woman in the world," he said, taking her hands.

"And you. Just, wow, you, Cal. Geez. Amazing." Tongue-tied, she couldn't describe what she managed to see. She shifted her head slightly to the side and got a good look at his gorgeous body. She made out abs, though they weren't washboard, but who cared? She ran her hand over the ridges. The muscles in his arms reminded her of the bear hugs he used to give.

Cal backed up to the bed, sat then lay down, pulling her on top of him. Arms and legs twined and untwined. Mouths explored. Cal sat up and flipped Giselle over and underneath him. Like a rag doll, she flopped this way or that. She trapped him between her legs.

"I've got you now," she boasted.

"Just where I wanted to be." He slid down, kissing her neck and moving south.

His lips left a hot trail down her chest, stopping between her breasts then paying attention to each one. When he tugged gently on each nipple with his teeth, she arched, sensation traveling straight to her core.

"When you do that," she mumbled.

"What? When I do that, what?" He raised his head.

"Damn, don't stop!"

His laugh rumbled deep in his chest, vibrating against her belly. Sliding down farther, his fingers made contact with her slit.

"Oh crap!" she hollered.

"Did I hurt you?"

"No, no, and don't stop. Please!" she begged.

He explored with his hands and his eyes before his mouth got in the act. Swirling his tongue over her hot flesh drove her crazy. Tension coiled inside her, tightening with every touch of his gifted tongue. When he slipped a finger inside her, the intensity ratcheted up, and an orgasm grew.

"If you don't... I'm gonna..." she sputtered.

He chuckled. "Go ahead. Do it. Come for me, baby." He lowered his head and continued to drive her wild. She fisted the sheet with both hands as her eyes shut and the heat in her exploded into a giant orgasm. Cal didn't stop until sensitivity turned pleasure into pain. She held up a hand.

"You done?"

"Finished. Completed. Amazed," she said.

"My turn." Cal jumped off the bed and snatched his pants from the floor. He plucked a condom from his wallet resting in the back pocket and returned to her side. He tore it open with his teeth then rolled it down his rock-hard dick. Giselle closed her fingers around him, staring.

"Can you see it?"

She nodded. "But even better, I can feel it. Gonna start calling you Man of Steel."

He laughed. "Now lie back and enjoy round two," he said, nudging her down.

This was what she'd been hankering for, waiting for, dreaming about—being physically connected to him again. He pushed up on his knees, rubbed himself against her to get some lubrication then plunged in.

She moaned, her head back, her tongue coating her lips. "Oh, Cal. Yes! Yes!"

CAL STARED AT HER FACE, beautiful in ecstasy. Her long, black lashes fanned out on her cheek, a delicate pink blush shaded her cheeks, and her lips turned rosy from being kissed. Oh God, it felt so damn good to be inside her. She was so tight, he almost panicked that he'd come too soon. He wanted her to climax again before he did.

He wanted to give her the moon, in bed and out. Could showering her with love and happiness make up for the pain he'd caused and the years they'd missed? He was here, in her bed, making love to her, committing every touch, every kiss to memory. He needed her, had always needed her, her love, her unquestioning devotion, to make him whole.

As he pumped away, watching her expression, his body jumped awake as if it had been sleeping since he'd last loved her. His skin sparked to the touch of her fingertips, the brush of her hard nipples against his chest. Passion grew inside him as control gradually slipped away.

He pumped into her harder and faster. He had to make her come before he did. His heart raced as the pressure mounted.

"Oh God, Cal!" she shouted, her hips rising, her inner muscles clenching and releasing, clenching and releasing his dick. Holy shit, nothing ever felt so good. Her hips kept a rhythm with his as he bent to kiss her. Cal thrust in again and again, his balls tightened, and he blew his wad. A huge groan, sounding like "Zell", his long-ago nickname for her, escaped his throat. Sweat broke out on his forehead and chest. He bent his head to touch hers. Her chest heaved.

"Zell, amazing," was all he could choke out. His eyes drifted shut.

She combed her fingers through his hair and kissed his neck. "My darling Cal. Stupendous," she whispered, close to his ear.

He'd touched supreme happiness and had no words to question what had occurred. Warm and soft beneath him, he could lie like this forever. Finally, he pulled out of her and dragged himself off the bed to head to the bathroom. He flushed the condom and returned to her. She lay naked and open to his eyes, looking beautiful.

"A well-loved woman," he said.

"Yes. Oh yes."

He slid next to her on the bed and pulled up the bedclothes, covering her first. Slipping one arm beneath her, he drew her close, resting against his chest. After smoothing her hair, he kissed it and pulled the blankets to her shoulder.

Shutting his eyes, he focused on her sweet scent, the lily of the valley, and the awesome aroma of sex. He snaked his free arm around her, opening his hand and resting his palm on her back. Her warmth heated him and the sheets. Pleasure and comfort soothed him.

"You belong to me, Zell. Always have and always will."

"Uh-huh." Her breathing evening out. He could tell she was asleep, lying on him, totally relaxed, trusting him the way she used to.

He grinned, satisfaction still coursing through his veins. She'd given him her body, but did he have her heart, her love? *One step at a time.* Although the physical had been jaw-dropping, fantastic, amazing sex, he knew it wasn't only about making love for either of them. He wanted more, and he guessed so did she.

She shifted her position, snaking her arm around his waist, pressing her breasts into his chest. The feel of her against him both aroused and calmed him. The last few years working and raising Bobby alone had taken their toll on Cal. He'd been gruff with the world, always tired, always second-guessing what to do with his son, and fighting solitude.

If it was true Giselle was back in his life, then that rough armor he'd used to guard his heart would melt away. Did he dare to hope to become a whole man, a husband, lover, and father? Could he count on her? Could he believe her? Damn right he could.

She mumbled something he couldn't understand. Her lips brushed his chest, and she shifted position again. Reaching out, she fumbled around, finally connecting with the lamp, switching it off.

He stroked her hair and let his eyes drift shut. He'd simply float on a cloud of happiness until morning, when reality would awaken again. Together, they could face anything—her disability, raising a child together, and maybe even having another one.

Cal grinned. Exhaustion crept through him, but he slept with a smile.

GISELLE TOSSED, HER mind restless, grappling with a troubling dream. When she came in contact with Cal, she started awake.

"Wha? Who? Who are you?" she said, her voice hazy.

"It's me. Cal."

"Cal?"

"You all right?" he asked, his deep voice husky.

"Uh-huh. Bad dream."

"Come here," he said, reaching for her. After she slid closer, he tucked her head into his shoulder and draped his arm around her. She snuggled into him. His chest hair tickled her nose. Cal pulled the blanket up to her neck.

"It's cold in here," he remarked.

"Always," she replied.

Giselle's mind relaxed. She fell back to sleep quickly and remained quiet until five. Rolling over on her stomach, she yawned. It was pitch-black outside. She dozed on and off for an hour. Cal snored softly. He rolled onto his side and tossed an arm over her chest. His hand landed on her breast, the fingers closing around it.

Still asleep, he squeezed it then his fingers opened. Desire awoke, she wanted more. Torn between wanting to luxuriate in his warm bear-like presence and wanting to make love, she mentally examined the pros and cons of both before deciding on a more aggressive approach. Sliding her fingers down his body, she stopped at his groin.

Easing the covers down, she exposed him. He stirred, reaching for the blanket. Giselle leaned over and took his partially erect dick into her mouth.

"What the hell?" He bolted upright.

She sat up. "Good morning. Just a little friendly wake-up call," she said and returned her attentions to him.

"Oh my God. You scared the shit out of me." He rubbed his stubbly face. "But don't let me interrupt you."

She giggled, sending vibrations through him. When Giselle pushed up on her knees to get a better angle, a hand patted her butt. She gasped when a finger entered her. Then another. Heat shot through her as Cal moved his hand.

"Oh God. You'd better stop," he said, easing her away. "Early morning. Be right back."

He pushed to his feet and hightailed it to the bathroom, stopping on the way back to pluck a condom from his pants pocket.

"You had more than one? Wasn't that a bit optimistic?"

He stared at her for a second then a shit-eating grin spread across his face. "I had a feeling things might go this way."

"You assumed you'd spend the night with me? Isn't that a bit arrogant?"

"Not assumed. Hoped. Prayed. Wished."

She laughed.

Cal pulled her close. "Come on, honey, don't be mad because I wanted to make love to you."

His tender words, his kneading the muscles in her neck and shoulder calmed her. Sitting up, she snaked her arms around his waist and kissed his pecs.

"What if I had come unprepared? We'd be two damn frustrated people right now."

"You have a point."

He tilted her chin up, staring into her eyes. "I love you, Zell. Let me show you how much." He eased her back down on the bed then knelt beside her. His eyes feasted on her, while his fingertips smoothed over her skin, from her chest to her thighs.

"You are so beautiful. Amazing."

She reached up to cup his cheek. "I love you, too, Cal. Always have."

He lay down on the bed. She sat up and slung one leg over his hips. He grasped her hips and eased her down on his erect dick. She shut her eyes and closed her legs around his body.

"I want to see you, watch you," he said, steadying her.

A blush started on her chest and stole all the way up to her cheeks.

"Don't be shy. It's me," he said.

She flattened her palms on his pecs and leaned down to kiss him. He slid his hands up her sides to cup her breasts. Giselle groaned and moved her hips. Heat flashed out from his dick to the rest of his body.

Giselle moved faster, he gripped her waist again, watching her breasts bob up and down. His thumbs caressed the smooth skin of her belly while his fingertips pressed into her back muscles.

"You have a great body," he said.

"Me? You're the one," she replied, breathless.

He took control, ramping up the speed. Giselle threw her head back, her eyes closed, and her mouth open slightly. Watching her climax shot the flames inside him from smokin' to wildfire.

As she found her release, his balls tightened, and he followed her, calling out "Zell" as he found completion. She crumpled, falling softly to his chest, her calves still clinging to him. He embraced her in a bear hug, kissing the top of her head and scraping his short stubble against her hair.

"Zell, baby."

"Wow," came the reply, muffled by his neck.

"Yeah."

They lay in each other's arms without speaking. Like old times, Cal fell right into the comfort zone they had shared years ago. He wished they could stay like this all day, all weekend, until the end of time.

Interrupted by a text from his father, Cal sighed as he read.

Get dressed, Romeo. We'll be there in an hour.

AT THE BREAKFAST TABLE, sipping coffee, Giselle slipped her hand over Cal's. Reluctant to break the dream-like quality of their time together, she had to interrupt their easy silence.

"What do we do now?" she asked.

Cal raised his gaze from the cinnamon bun on his plate. "That depends. What do you want?"

"I want to be with you."

"And I feel the same." He took a big bite.

"What about Bobby?"

Cal chewed, his expression thoughtful.

"We have to tell him," she said.

"I think he'd be overjoyed if you moved in."

"Moved in?" her eyebrows jumped.

"That's what being together means. Doesn't it?"

"Not full-time. Not right away. Shouldn't we ease into this?" she asked.

"Why? We've already wasted too many years being apart."

"I know. But I have things to figure out. Like where my life's going." She took a sip of her coffee.

"Your life is going in tandem with mine. What's wrong with that?"

"It's not enough. I can't just stop working, have no career, nothing to call my own."

"You can call Bobby and me your own."

She laughed. "As delightful as that is, it isn't quite what I had in mind."

Cal finished his food and rubbed his chin. "How about you stay with me on weekends until you're ready to make it full-time."

"Weekends works for me."

"Good." He raised her hand to his lips.

But she wondered, would full-time mean marriage? She didn't want to be the live-in girlfriend, the one who could get dropped like a hot coal if he felt like it. She wanted, no needed, a commitment. But she couldn't exactly propose to him, could she? Besides, there was Bobby to consider. What if he didn't take to it as well as Cal expected? What if he got jealous or acted out? And how would she feel waking up in Cal's bed in front of his son?"

"What?" he asked.

"Huh?" No longer lost in thought, she looked up.

"Something's going on in that pretty head. What is it?"

"Just wondering how this is going to work with Bobby."

"He'll be happy to have you as his mother."

"But as a weekend guest, I won't be his mother, will I?"

Cal's brows knitted. "Guess not. Hadn't thought about that."

"I'd be embarrassed to have him walk in on us in bed."

"We'll teach him to knock."

"You know what I mean." She got up to get a refill. "More coffee?"

"Sure." Cal handed her his cup.

She hung her pinky over the side. When the coffee met her finger, the mug was full.

Cal checked his watch. "Time to get dressed. They'll be home in half an hour."

Together, they headed for the bedroom and quickly donned their clothes from the night before. With Cal's arm slung over her shoulder, she strode across the lawn to his house. He arranged some logs and lit a fire. A lazy Sunday with Bobby and Cal warmed her heart.

The doorbell rang. When Cal opened it. Bobby came flying in, full of energy and recounting all the great activities he did with his grandparents.

"Then we made pipe-cleaner men. And I helped Grandma bake molasses cookies. And Grandpa and I brought in wood," the boy rattled on. He turned and spied Giselle. "Giselle." He ran to her, throwing his arms around her.

She hugged him. Betty Morrison shot her a knowing smile. "How nice to see you two together."

"How would you feel if Giselle stayed with us every weekend?" Cal asked.

"Can she? Really?" the boy asked.

Cal nodded.

Bobby let out a war whoop and twirled and twirled until dizziness brought him down.

Chuckling, Cal's father warmed himself by the fire. Betty approached Giselle.

"Do you have plans for Christmas? If not, why don't you join us? We'd love to have you. Spend the day. Can you?"

Tears pricked at the backs of her eyes. She'd been moping around about Christmas, barely fighting off a full-scale pity party. She glanced at Cal and his son. Bobby jumped up.

"Can you? Huh? Can you? Please?"

She laughed. "Okay. You twisted my arm, Bobby."

"No, I didn't, honest."

"That's just an expression, Son. It means you convinced her," Cal explained.

"Oh. It's good, right?"

"Right," Cal replied.

Al toted Bobby's backpack to his room.

"Why don't you come by for breakfast. Say nine? And stay through dinner," Betty asked.

"Great! I was dreading Christmas alone."

"Good, then. That's settled." Betty hugged her.

Cal eased an arm around Giselle, and she leaned against him. Happiness filled her veins. What better Christmas present could there be?

"Are you gonna bring the talking books with you?" Bobby asked.

"Sure," she said.

"Let's go get you packed up." Cal headed for the door.

"Can I come?" Bobby asked.

"Of course," Giselle told him.

With Cal in the middle, holding hands on both sides, the trio marched across the street. He took the keys from her and unlocked the door.

"I don't need much if I'm coming home tomorrow," she said, absently.

"Maybe you should move in, permanently," Cal ventured, as he raised his eyebrows.

"Now?"

"Haven't we waited long enough?" Cal asked.

Giselle hesitated.

"Can I have a cookie?" Bobby asked.

"Sure," she said. "If it's okay with your father."

"Fine," Cal said.

Giselle shifted her weight and stared at the floor.

"Okay. I'll stop pushing." Cal approached her.

"I need to get there on my own. There are so many things to deal with now," she said.

"I'll try to be patient. Let's get you packed." Cal headed for her bedroom.

They hadn't had time to make the bed. The sight of the rumpled sheets gave her goose bumps.

"I'll check on Bobby. Throw some stuff in a bag and let's go home," Cal said, screeching to a halt by the dresser.

Home. God that word sounded good to her.

He blushed and gazed at his hands. "I mean, my place."

She reached over and squeezed his arm. "Home," she said, before turning away. He was gone in a flash, calling his son's name. As she dropped garments and toiletry articles in a small valise, Giselle wondered what this meant. While she wanted to be with Cal and Bobby, it had happened so fast she could hardly catch her breath. And what about Cal's son? How would he adjust? Sure, he said he wanted a mother, but what would happen if she laid down the law with him? What did Giselle know about being a mother? Nothing.

Her stomach clenched. Her phone rang. It was Aunt Julia.

"Hi, sweetie. Just calling to find out your plans before I take off for the city."

"I'm spending Christmas Day with Cal and his family."

"You are? That's fabulous. Isn't it kind of sudden?"

"Maybe."

"Are you happy?"

"I am."

"Then that's all that counts," Julia replied.

"I'm going to be staying at Cal's on weekends," Giselle blurted out.

"Oh, Giselle! I'm so happy for you. Honestly, sweetie, you two belong together. Guess this is going to be a very merry Christmas."

She smiled. "I guess so."

"I wish your mom was here. She always liked Cal."

"She did. She was right."

"All is forgiven?" Julia asked.

"Guess so."

"Time will take care of it. No worries. Gotta catch my bus. Merry Christmas, love," Julia said.

"Merry Christmas, Aunt Julia," Giselle replied.

She tucked the phone into her purse and grinned. Her mother would be happy. Cal poked his head in with Bobby at his side, munching on a cookie.

"Ready?" Cal asked, picking up her suitcase.

"Yep."

The threesome made tracks back to Cal's house. Giselle pushed doubts out of her mind. Envisioning the nights she'd spend with Cal sent a shiver up her spine. Was he the best gift a woman could get for Christmas, or would sudden motherhood be beyond her grasp?

Chapter Twelve

Cal's nerves kicked up when he carried Giselle's bag into the bedroom. Was this real? Had she agreed to almost move in with him? Was he the luckiest man on Earth, or would she change her mind and crap out on him in a day, a week, a month? He frowned.

"Daddy, Giselle is having a sleep over in my room," a small voice behind him caught his attention.

Cal chuckled. "I'm afraid not, Son. She's a grown up. She'll stay in my room."

Bobby's face clouded over. He thrust out his lower lip and stomped his foot. "No fair!"

Standing in the doorway, Giselle blushed. Cal glanced at her and shrugged. She approached the boy, kneeling down and touching his shoulder.

"Bobby, you know I care for you. But I care for your father, too. In the way two grown-ups do. It's different. But I'll be spending lots of time with you."

"Will you bring the talking books into my room?"

"Good idea. We can listen to them there."

The boy turned his scowling face to his father. "And Daddy can't come. Just you and me."

Giselle's eyebrows shot up. Cal stifled a grin, lowered his gaze, and grabbed all the self-control he had to keep a straight face.

"It's okay. You and Giselle can listen to the talking books without me. I respect that."

"You can't come in. I'm gonna close the door," Bobby said, his voice firm, his lips compressed into a frown.

Cal raised his hands to show his palms. "She'll be all yours, then."

"Good." The boy stomped into his room and shut the door. The sound of muffled crying came through the door. Giselle moved toward Bobby's room, but Cal put his hand on her arm and stopped her.

"I'll go." He knocked on the door.

"Go away!" came the response.

"It's me, Bobby. Can I come in?" Cal asked.

"No!"

"Please?"

"No!"

"Aw, come on. If you let me in, I'll let you pick the movie tonight."

"No! You have to let me pick the next five times."

"Okay. It's a deal."

The knob turned slowly. A sad, tear-stained face greeted the adults. Cal entered. He picked up his son and flopped down on the bed, leaving the door open. Giselle lurked in the doorway.

Hugging Bobby, Cal kissed the boy's head and held him on his chest.

"You love Giselle, don't you?"

The boy nodded. He rubbed the collar of Cal's flannel shirt between his fingers.

"I love her, too." Cal stroked his son's head.

"You do?"

"I've loved her for a long time."

"You have?"

"Yep."

"I want her to be my mother."

"So do I."

"You do?" the boy asked.

A gasp came from the doorway. Cal kept his gaze on his son.

"I do. Do you think I should ask her to marry me?"

The boy nodded.

"I thought so."

"Then she can live here all the time?" Bobby asked.

"Once we're married, she'll be here all the time. Sleeping in my room, being your mother and my wife."

"Yes!" the boy replied.

"Good. I'm glad you agree. Because I do, too. Now we just have to ask her," Cal said.

"Will you ask her, Daddy?"

"I will if you back me up."

A soft cry and a sniffle came from across the room. Cal glanced at Giselle. She wiped tears off her cheeks with her fingers.

Bobby sat up. "Giselle's crying." He turned to his father. "Did you make her cry?"

"I don't think so."

"No, he didn't. These are happy tears," she said.

"Daddy, ask her." Bobby yanked on his father's sleeve.

Cal took the boy by the shoulders and set him down then pushed to his feet. He brushed himself off, combed his hair back from his forehead with his fingers, cleared his throat, coughed, and smiled.

"Well, Giselle?"

"Well what?" she shot back at him, sporting a saucy grin.

He reached into his back pocket and dropped down to one knee. "Will you marry me?"

"Us, Daddy," Bobby whispered in his father's ear.

"Will you marry us?" Cal opened the box and offered her a sparkly one-carat diamond ring.

Giselle covered her mouth with her hands and took a deep breath.

"Well?" Bobby asked.

She nodded but didn't speak.

"I'm afraid I can't hear you," Cal said, chuckling.

"Yes," she squeaked out.

Bobby took the ring out of the box, grabbed her hand, and put it in her palm.

"We'll get it resized." Cal rose to his feet.

"Where did you get this? When? How did you know?"

He stopped in front of her, took her chin between his fingers, raised her face to his. "I bought it six years ago, before you told me you were leaving."

She gasped again, and her mouth fell open. "You've held on to it all this time?"

"Yep." He took the ring and slipped it on her finger. It was a little big.

"Oh, Cal," she managed to whisper.

He took her in his arms and kissed her. Giselle wound her arms around his neck and molded her body to his.

"Yuck!!" Bobby yelled and ran from the room. The lovers broke, laughing and followed.

The deed had been done. The relationship hit the fast track. Cal took a deep breath. The butterflies in his stomach calmed down. She was his now, well, almost his, and he prayed it would last.

GISELLE SAT AT THE kitchen table while Bobby watched a movie. Stunned by the proposal and afraid to be happy, she simply stared out the window. Cal joined her, setting a mug of hot coffee in front of her.

"You don't look happy." He took a sip.

"I am. Very happy." She twisted the loose ring on her finger.

"You don't sound happy, either."

"If I'm going to be living here, I need to learn this kitchen," she said, rising.

"My house is bigger, but if you want to move into yours, we can do that."

She shook her head. "Doesn't make sense." She got up close to the stove and bent over, studying the controls. "Gas stove?"

"Yep."

"That won't work for me. I can't have gas."

"Why?"

"Because I might not see the flame and start a fire."

"We'll buy an electric tomorrow. I'll take you shopping."

Giselle faced him. "There are going to be a lot of things that need to be different. Are you sure you want to do this?"

"Do what? Marry you? Never been more sure of anything in my life. So things have to be different? We'll fix whatever we can, change what we can't fix. You can set up the talking microwave here."

She smiled. Could she live a regular life? It had been her biggest question since her sight weakened. A regular life, marriage, kids, a home—all the things she's always wanted. Was it possible she'd have those with Cal and Bobby? If so, then there would only be one thing missing—a career. But she'd have to figure it out on her own. Cal couldn't wave a magic wand and produce the perfect job.

"Drink." He pushed the drink closer.

Giselle wrapped both hands around the large mug and lifted it to her lips. The aromatic brew tasted good. Words from Aunt Julia rang in her head. *One step at a time.*

"What about dinner?"

"I thought we could make it together. I can help you find your way around the kitchen."

"We need to keep things in their place. If we do, I'll learn where everything is, and you'll never know I can't see well."

"Okay, then. Done. And I'll tell Bobby, too." His hand slid over hers. "It's going to be all right. We'll get it done."

"I hope so. I want this to work. Us. You, me, and Bobby. It's what I've always wanted."

"Then it'll happen." He raised her hand to his lips.

Bobby sauntered in. "Popcorn?"

"Coming up," Cal said, rising and opening a cabinet door. He popped it in the microwave and, when it was done, filled a small bowl. Bobby carried it back to the living room.

Cal reached for her hand. "I've got some chopped meat, what do you want to do with it?"

Giselle rose. "Do you have onions? Tomato sauce or puree?"

"Over here." Cal pulled her toward the pantry then took her on a tour of the kitchen. She selected an onion, and Cal sliced it. Then, she took down a couple of cans of tomato sauce, and Cal ran them through the opener.

Working side by side, the couple brought dinner together so much faster than when Giselle worked alone. When they finished, the aroma of garlic and onions filled the air.

"Voila! Sloppy Joes," she said.

"Smells damn good," Cal said.

Bobby asked a ton of questions at dinner. While she fumfered around, looking for the right words, Cal cut right to the heart of things.

"Why is Giselle sleeping in your bed?" the boy asked.

Giselle sensed her face heat and searched for a good explanation when Cal piped up.

"Because adults who love each sleep in the same bed," Cal said.

"Is she going to be here every day?"

Again, words stuck in her throat.

"Not yet. Just weekends. Maybe Mondays, too. We're kinda gonna get used to each other first. After we're married, she'll move in full-time," Cal said.

After dinner, Cal washed the dishes while Giselle went with Bobby to listen to another chapter of the "talking book." When he was done, Cal joined them to prep Bobby for bed, and kissed him good night.

"When Giselle is here, you have to knock and wait for one of us to say 'come in,' okay?"

"Why?"

"Because she might be getting dressed or something. Ladies need privacy, get it?"

"Okay."

"You'll remember to knock and wait?"

The boy nodded.

"Good. Thanks." Cal pushed to his feet.

Giselle kissed Bobby on the forehead. The adults retired to the living room. Cal stretched his arms above his head and yawned.

"Bedtime," he said.

"It's eight o'clock. You can't really be tired?"

"Who said anything about being tired?"

She laughed and hugged him.

He bent his head to nibble on her neck. "You're not the least bit sleepy?"

"Now that you mention it, I am," Giselle said, feigning a yawn.

"IT'S WEIRD TO BE UNDRESSING with Bobby down the hall," she said.

"I know. We'll get used to it."

She parked her clothes on a nearby chair and climbed into bed. The sheets were cold.

"Hurry. It's freezing," she said, shivering.

Cal shot her a lusty look. "I'll take care of that."

After they made love, Giselle fell into an uneasy sleep with Cal's hand resting on her hip. Jolted awake by a nightmare, she panicked, forgetting where she was. Thrashing around, trying to get free from the tangled covers, she woke Cal.

"Giselle? You okay?"

"Huh? Wha?"

"It's me, Cal," he said, his voice deep and low. He reached out, but she shrank from him.

"Honey, it's okay. You're in my house." He flipped on the lamp next to the bed. "See?"

She trembled. "I didn't know where I was." Tears threatened.

Cal pulled her into his embrace. "It's all right, baby. You're here with me. You'll get used to my house. It'll be fine. Go back to sleep." He stroked her back, his tone calm and even.

After dousing the light, he settled back down into the bed, keeping her in his arms. She took a deep, shuddering breath before snuggling into him. His warmth, his scent soothed her. Even after all that had happened, she trusted Cal to keep her safe.

Intellectually, she understood about his marriage, but, emotionally, she worried he might find someone else. He swore he'd never even looked at another woman when they had been together. Knowledge of his fidelity when they were younger encouraged her to trust. She'd discarded her concern, declaring it irrational. Giselle wanted him and refused to let unfounded fears destroy what she so desperately needed—Cal Morrison's love.

She closed her fingers over his forearm and took another deep breath. His scent was all around her, coupled with a slightly sweet aftershave smell. She sighed and closed her eyes. Sleep overtook her quickly.

When the sun came up, something heavy landed on her.

"Oof!" Her eyes flew open.

A giggle greeted her.

"Bobby!" Cal yelled.

"What?"

The boy lay across Cal and Giselle. Cal picked him up and set him next to the bed.

"What did I say about knocking?"

"Where are your pajamas, Daddy?"

"Sometimes, adults don't wear pajamas."

As she bunched the sheet around her bare chest, Giselle felt the young boy's stare.

"Giselle doesn't have any, either."

"That's right. And you shouldn't barge in here like that. I told you, you have to knock and wait for the okay before coming in."

"But I wanted to surprise you," the boy wailed.

Giselle burst out laughing.

"You sure did. But no more. You'll have to wait outside while we get dressed."

"Okay," Bobby said, his voice low, his lip pouty.

Cal scampered, naked, across the room, ushering his son out and closing the door.

"I'm really sorry. I don't think that'll happen again."

"It's okay. He's curious." She threw the covers down and swung her feet over the side.

"Probably doesn't remember much about his mom living here," Cal said.

Giselle stopped. "How sad!"

"He needs you. And so do I." He cupped her cheek and brushed her lips with his.

She dressed quickly and went searching for the boy. He sat on the living room floor, still in his pj's, playing with a dump truck. He looked up when she entered.

"Can I have pancakes?"

Cal came up right behind her. "Pancakes are for weekends. Let's get you dressed. It's hot cereal today."

Bobby made a face. "Giselle makes good pancakes."

"Yes, she does. And we'll have them on Saturday morning. Giddy yup. We don't want to be late for school," he said, hustling his son from the room.

Giselle hunted around the kitchen, looking for coffee. One glance at the complex coffeemaker and she gave up. She plopped down on a chair at the kitchen table, frustrated. She had a lot to learn about where things were and the guys' morning routine.

Within fifteen minutes, Cal returned with his son dressed.

"You need to show me how to make coffee," she said.

"Don't worry about it," Cal said. "I'll get it started."

He bustled about the kitchen, fixing coffee and getting a dish of hot oatmeal with brown sugar ready.

"Do you like oatmeal?" he asked her.

"Yes."

"Good." Cal slapped a heaping serving spoon of the stuff into three dishes. He sprinkled raisins on them, added brown sugar and a dash of milk, and brought them to the table. Bobby chattered on about school and who he wanted to play with on the playground.

Pushing aside her feeling of helplessness, Giselle ate her food and sipped coffee, enjoying the sweet aromas filling the air and the banter between father and son.

"So, who are you playing with today?" Cal asked.

"Josh."

"Why him?"

"He doesn't have a mother, either. He doesn't ask me stuff about my mom."

The air became heavy, the silence like a blanket.

Cal cleared his throat. "Soon you'll have a mother."

"Yes. But not a real one."

Giselle's head snapped up.

"She is a real one," Cal insisted.

"Not the one who had me."

"No. And we can't bring her back. But Giselle'll be your mother in every other way."

Bobby lifted questioning eyes to her. She covered his hand with hers.

"Of course. I'll be your mother. I already love you the way a mother loves a son." She leaned over and kissed the top of his head.

He took another mouthful of food and stared at her. God, could she do this? Cal slipped his arm around her shoulders.

"I love Giselle. And she loves me. And you, too. We're still going to be a family. Just with one more member."

The boy chewed his food, his eyes darting from his father to Giselle and back again.

"You'll be my new mother?"

"Yes. I thought we'd talked about it. I want to be your mom. Very much."

Bobby put down his spoon, got up from the table, and threw himself into her embrace. She hugged him tight, tears dampening his dark hair.

"Time to go," Cal said, standing.

"Will you take me to school, Giselle?" Bobby asked.

"A good idea. We need to tell your teacher you have a new mom and she can pick you up from school sometimes." Cal pulled the boy's jacket down from a hook.

After bundling up, they tromped over to Pine Grove Elementary, two blocks away. Cal introduced Giselle to Miss Baker, Bobby's teacher.

"She's my new mom," Bobby piped up.

"Nice to meet you. Bobby contributes so much to the class," the teacher said.

"I'm glad to hear that," Giselle responded.

She bent down to place a kiss on the boy's head. Cal hugged him. After the children went inside, Cal took her hand. "Let's go shopping!" he said.

Chapter Thirteen

"Shopping?"

"For a new stove. New coffeemaker and Christmas stuff. Christmas is five days away!"

"Oh my God. Yes."

He held the door of his SUV open for her. They headed for the big stores in Willow Falls. Giselle sat back in the seat, listening to Cal talk about work. A feeling of peace flowed through her. Everything had happened so fast.

She'd been waiting to get on with her life for a long time. Wrestling with her disability, mastering it, had taken time. But she'd learned to compensate. She couldn't put life on hold forever. The only area still left to conquer was her career. What the hell would she do with her time? She chewed her lip. Cal fell silent, his attention focused on the road.

Time to make decisions. She stared out the window at the layer of snow in the woods and the bare branches. Where to begin? The first step hit her with clarity as she watched the frozen world around her whizz by. Shutting her eyes, she dozed until they pulled into the Walmart parking lot.

"Appliances first." Cal took her hand and led her to the right section.

They examined electric stoves and coffeemakers. After they found the easiest ones to use, Cal purchased both.

"Delivery tomorrow?" the man asked.

"That's fast," Cal remarked.

"Not many folks buying a new stove before the holiday."

"I need things for your parents," Giselle said.

"How about a book for dad?" Cal asked.

"Perfect. And a scarf for your mom?"

Cal nodded. They went from department to department, filling a cart.

"What does Bobby want most?" Giselle asked.

"Besides a new mother?"

"Stop." She shoved him gently in the shoulder.

"Okay, okay. The toy section," Cal said. "You already got him the Lego police station, right?"

"But that was as a friend. A neighbor. Not a mother," she protested.

"Okay. Waste your hard-earned money. I can't stop you." Cal smiled.

"A farm!" Giselle said. Pulling Cal, she spied wooden animals. "Let's get him everything he needs for his own farm."

"And who's going to clean up after the animals?" Cal chuckled.

"You're a Grinch, you know that? Come on. Help me. Let's see. We need pigs, cows, chickens, a barn."

"A farmer, his sexy wife, hmm," Cal said, rubbing his chin.

Giselle made a face at him. "Don't be gross. Help me."

He pulled her close for a quick kiss. "Sorry. Okay. Let's see, you've got the animals. Some fence. A farmhouse, maybe?"

"Yes!"

Together, they gathered everything Bobby would need for an amazing farm.

"We can wrap stuff separately, so he has a lot of presents." Giselle stuffed a small, toy chicken coop into the cart.

"Now you need to go away, so I can buy something for you." She gave him a little shove.

"Let's not exchange gifts this year."

"You've already bought me a stove, coffeemaker, and engagement ring. That lets you off the hook. But what have I got for you? Zip."

"You've given me yourself. That's enough. Besides, you're spending a small fortune on Bobby's farm."

"Please, Cal?" she begged.

He sighed, shrugged. "You have ten minutes. I'm going to look at car stuff."

"Okay."

Giselle made a beeline for the sporting goods department. After hunting for a bit, she found a salesman to help her. Then she spied—the perfect gift. It was something Cal had mentioned in passing. She put the best one in her basket then picked up her phone and called him. "Meet me at checkout."

She hid the gift for him when she paid.

"Turn around, Cal."

He shrugged and did as she asked.

They loaded their purchases in the car.

"Let's grab lunch at The Cozy Café before I pick up Bobby."

"Great."

They pulled up, and Cal glanced at the clock. "I don't have time. I'll grab something to go. You stay and take your time. Bobby and I'll come pick you up."

She nodded and took a seat at a table by the window overlooking Cedar Lake. Winter birds flew over the water, looking for a meal. She ordered an egg sandwich and coffee. When she finished, Laura Dailey joined her.

"How about a scone? Fresh from the oven?" Laura put down a plate.

"You tempt me."

"Rumor has it, you're engaged," Laura said, shyness never being one of her shortcomings.

Giselle held out her left hand. "It's true."

"Cal?"

"Who else?"

"Rumor also said you'd been stepping out with Chris, Stryker West's chauffeur."

"Nope. He was only driving me over to the thrift shop."

"Congratulations. All I can say is, 'bout time." Laura laughed. Giselle smiled.

"What are you gonna do now? Re-open the thrift shop?"

"No. I don't really know what I'm going to do. I can't decide where my life is going."

"You'll be a wife and mother. Should keep you pretty busy," Laura replied.

"It's not enough for me. I need to work. Make my own money. Do something with my life outside of Cal and Bobby."

"Any ideas?"

"I'm coming up empty," Giselle said. "You?"

Laura shook her head. A timer went off, and the baker pushed to her feet. "Gotta go. You'll figure it out. You'll see."

The door opened, and Chris entered. Giselle flagged him over.

"Congratulations on your engagement. I see things have worked out," he said.

"Thank you. Yes. Want company?"

"Sure." He placed his order.

"Chris, can I ask you a favor?"

"Of course."

When he finished eating, they went out to his car. Giselle called Cal and told her Chris would drive her home. The fancy vehicle pulled up in front of the thrift shop. Giselle got out. Chris kept the motor running. She made her way up the steps. Fishing around in her bag, she found the metal sign. She hung it on the front of the store then returned to the car.

She shut the door and sighed.

"For sale?" Chris asked, turning toward her.

CAL DIDN'T LIKE IT that Giselle hitched a ride home with Chris. He'd said he'd be back. Why didn't she wait? Why did she go with that guy? A voice in his head, directly from his mother's heart, told him to shut up and let it go. Afterall, she was engaged to Cal. No reason to worry about Chris, right?

He brought Bobby home and made him a snack.

"Where's Giselle?"

"She's getting a ride home from The Cozy Café with a friend," Cal said. *Yeah, a friend. Guy's probably got the hots for her and she doesn't even know it.*

Bobby went outside to play on the swings. The sun tempered the cold air enough so the boy could get exercise and work his sillies out. Cal watched from the kitchen window as he prepared ingredients for a Crock-Pot stew.

The doorbell reminded him he hadn't given Giselle a key. He opened the door, and she stopped to wave at Chris before crossing the threshold.

"I need to give you a key," Cal said. "Do you have to get a ride with him?" Unable to keep a note of irritation and jealousy out of his voice, he wanted to kick himself. Opening the drawer in the small stand in the foyer, he rummaged around for a spare key.

"Who? Chris?"

"I shouldn't have said anything."

"You jealous?" she asked, her eyebrows rising.

Cal sensed heat in his face as he handed her the key. "Not really."

"Yes, you are." She stepped closer and kissed him. "Don't be jealous. We're engaged. I'm not interested in anyone else."

He grinned. "As long as you remember you belong to me."

"Do I?" she asked, bristling.

Instead of answering with words, he snaked his arm around her waist, pulling her to him, and planted a passionate kiss. She softened against him. They stood together for a moment before he let her go and made his way to the kitchen. She followed. "Want me to put the key on your keychain?"

"How did you guess?" She felt around in her purse until she found it.

While he peered out the window, checking on his son, Cal added the new key. Bobby's friend, Josh, had joined him. The two boys swung up and down. Cal put the top on the Crock-Pot and turned it on. He slung his arm around Giselle's shoulders, leaning on her. She rested her head against him.

"It's okay if Santa skips me this year. I've already got everything I want." He nuzzled her neck.

"Me, too."

In twenty minutes, two frozen little boys entered the warm kitchen. Cal made a fire. The boys took off their snowy boots and warm jackets then munched on popcorn by the crackling logs. The aroma of stew cooking filled the air. Giselle's stomach rumbled.

"Hey, this is your house, too. If you're hungry, please raid the fridge," Cal said.

"I got books that talk," Bobby said.

"Books don't talk. You gotta read 'em," Josh replied.

"Yeah? I got books that talk. Come on. I'll show you. Giselle, can I put on a book?"

"Let me do it, Bobby. Which one do you want?" She disappeared into the bedroom with the boys.

Cal stretched his legs, resting his feet on the coffee table, and opened the newspaper. He read through, absorbing the news and looking for new places to pitch his business. He never knew where he'd find someone who needed tree work or plowing.

The faint sounds of an adult male voice drew his attention. He grinned and shook his head at his initial response. His nerves were cocked and ready. It was only the audiobook.

"Cal. Slow down," he told himself.

His life changes had raced ahead like a car in the Indy 500. Maybe they needed to slow things a bit. Was he having trouble switching gears from single father to family man? He didn't want to put the brakes on his relationship. He'd finally jump-started his life, and it was about time! Why not get it up to speed?

What would he gain? He argued with himself.

Maybe more time to adjust to things being different?

He'd have to adjust faster.

What about Giselle? She seemed to be okay. Except for last night when she almost had a heart attack.

He rubbed the back of his neck. Yeah. Getting used to a new house took time. He'd have to be patient, and she'd have to be determined.

What about Bobby? He'd have to learn new rules. Couldn't have him bustin' in on Cal and Giselle getting undressed or making love. The boy said he wanted a new mother, but could he make the changes that required?

People had remarked to Cal how well he and Bobby got along, just the two of them. But it had been a façade. Loneliness had burned in his belly. Not normally a jealous man, envy had heated his face at school and town events as he watched loving husbands and wives with their kids. When the men took their cans of beer to the lake to fish for an hour while the women watched the children, anger had flared up inside Cal. Sure, he could have left Bobby with his grandparents, but it wouldn't have been the same. If Jane hadn't been so reckless, she'd have been there and life would have been different.

Cal put the paper down and stared out the window. With limited eyesight, could Giselle mind Bobby while Cal was at work? She had had charge of him already and it worked. He sighed. Already, the jealousy in him lessened. He looked forward to having his wife by his side at parent-teacher conferences, like so many other fathers. Giselle filled his home with the love that had been missing for a long time. Would she stay?

AFTER DINNER, THEY settled Bobby in bed and lounged on the sofa, drinking tea. Cal's mother called. He untangled himself from his fiancée and picked up the phone.

"What did you do?" came her accusing voice.

"What?"

"What did you do to Giselle?"

"Nothing. I asked her to marry me, and she said 'yes.'"

"Bull. Don't pull your innocent act on me, Calvin Joseph Morrison."

Uh-oh. When his mom used his full name, Cal knew he was in trouble. "Ma, I have no idea what you're talking about."

"Like you don't know Giselle put a For Sale sign up on the thrift shop today?"

"What?"

"You mean you didn't know?"

"No, I didn't."

"People're pretty upset. We need that place. Did you make her do it?"

"Ma, you oughta know by now I can't make her do anything."

"Don't get cute with me. You'd better get to the bottom of this and fix it. We need that shop," Betty said then paused. "And she needs to run it."

"I'll pass along your opinion. Let me look into it."

"And get back to me?"

"I will. Promise."

The conversation ended. Cal narrowed his eyes and faced Giselle.

"Are you selling the thrift shop?"

"Boy, news travels fast in Pine Grove."

"Is that a 'yes'?"

She nodded.

"Why?"

"Because I can't run it. And it's too expensive to keep open just for Santa's Thrift Shop, once a year. The taxes, electricity, heat, and stuff. I need to find something to do, a career. I don't have a clue, right now. But I can't do the thrift shop."

"Why not? You had people helping you."

"I need to keep books, do all the writing stuff that comes with owning a store. Work a computer. That's probably out of the question for me."

"I'll help. You had help this year."

"That's this year. I don't want to be beholden to people. You can't ask someone to volunteer to help you run your business. I need to be able to pay employees. Most of my inventory went out during Santa's Thrift Shop. I can't afford to buy more."

Cal rubbed the pad of his thumb over the back of her hand. "Mom's pretty upset. And I'll bet she's not the only one."

Giselle pushed to her feet. "I can't help it. Of course I'd want to keep it open. It never does much business, but Mom and I liked working there. People would stop by to visit. We made sales every week. Before Jess Lennox married Stryker, she was a regular there."

"There are a lot of people here who can't afford new stuff," Cal said.

"I know. I liked helping out. But I simply can't do it anymore. And I need to make money. The money from selling my parents' house won't last forever."

"You're going to be my wife. You don't need money. We do okay. I'm not a rich man, but, during the season, I do pretty well. Enough to pay for the house, food, clothes. Whatever we need."

"Whatever you and Bobby need. But now there'll be three of us. Things change. Besides, I'm used to having my own money. I want to work, not just sit around all day. Vacuum and cook. I need to have something that's mine."

"And the thrift shop was it." Cal slowly nodded his head.

"Yes. Before. When I had good eyesight."

"If you sell it, what are you going to do?"

She sank next to him on the sofa and folded her arms across her chest. "I don't know."

"Do you have to sell it now?"

"I don't imagine it's going to get snapped up by anyone. It might take a long time to sell."

"I see." He rubbed his chin.

"So, I put the sign up. I haven't talked to a real estate agent yet."

"Hmm. Okay. How about waiting until after the holidays?"

"I guess. Don't imagine anyone's looking to buy a store now anyway."

"Let's take the sign down. Just for now," he said.

"Okay."

"I'll drive you over there tomorrow."

"All right. I'm tired. I'm going to bed." She rose and headed for the bedroom.

"I'll be there in a minute," Cal said, snatching up his phone. He texted his mother.

Cal: *She's backing off until after the holidays. You have ten days to do something.*

Mom: *That isn't much time.*

Cal: *It's the best I could do.*

Mom: *Okay. I'll come up with something.*

Cal closed his phone and headed for the bedroom. It was dark. He slipped off his clothes and climbed in next to Giselle's luscious body. She was already asleep. He cuddled next to her and closed his eyes. *Damn. Life complications set in already.*

He sighed, tucking his arm around her. Giselle was worth it.

GISELLE SLEPT SOUNDLY. A knock on the door awoke her.

"Just a minute," came a sleepy voice next to her.

Giselle popped out of bed, grabbed a nightgown she'd left on the chair, and slipped it over her head.

"Ready?" Cal mumbled, yawning and scratching his chest.

She nodded.

"Come in."

A small tornado in the form of a five-year-old boy flew into the room, racing around and leaping on the bed, all energy and smiles. Cal hugged him to his chest and growled in his ear. Bobby shrieked with laughter.

"Oh no! Hairy monster!" Bobby yelled, while Cal pretended to feast on his son's neck.

Giselle wrapped a robe around her and watched. She giggled along with the men as they wrestled and tussled together. Finally, Cal stopped, and Bobby quieted down. The boy looked so small in his father's strong arms. He waved Giselle over. She shook her head.

"Get over here." Cal's eyes gleamed with mischief.

"It's her turn!" Bobby hollered.

"Oh no," she said, inching nearer to the door.

Cal tossed Bobby on the other side of the bed, swung his legs over, and pulled on his boxers. She headed for the door and was out and making tracks to the living room with Cal right behind, and Bobby bringing up the rear. Fortunately, Bobby had picked up his toys and she had a clear path to the dining room.

"Catch her, Daddy! Catch her!"

Giselle made it to the round dining room table. She and Cal faced off. He grinned, faking one way and going the other to trap her in his embrace.

"Daddy won!" Bobby yelled, hopping up and down.

"I've got you now. You're my prisoner!"

"No, no," she begged, feigning fear.

Cal buried his face in her neck then angled her chin up for a possessive kiss. Bobby stopped and watched as his father's hungry mouth ravaged Giselle's. She wound her arms around his neck. The distant sound of the alarm clock going off brought them back to Earth.

Giselle sensed heat in her cheeks as she peeked over at Bobby.

"Kissing. Yuck!" He scrunched up his face.

Cal dropped his arms and smiled at her. "How about eggs and raisin toast?"

"Raisin toast? Yes!" Bobby sprinted to the kitchen.

Giselle only bumped into Cal about four times whizzing around the kitchen. She'd mastered the new, simple coffeemaker. While Cal whipped up eggs, she manned the toaster. Cal poured juice, and Bobby got the butter from the fridge.

After breakfast, getting dressed, and taking Bobby to school for his last day before the holiday, Cal and Giselle walked hand in hand back to the house.

"Christmas Eve is tomorrow night," he said.

"Do they still have the carolers?" she asked.

"Oh yes. And the horse and cart ride down Main Street. Homer's sells hot chocolate and cider from a table right in front of the restaurant.

"Can we go?"

"Wouldn't miss it. Bobby loves it."

"And you?" she asked.

"Me, too." He squeezed her hand.

"It's so nice of your parents to include me for Christmas."

"You're family now."

His words warmed her heart. She'd hardly had time to think about Christmas. When she sold her parents' house, it had been emotionally painful to clear out the attic and go through all the Christmas decorations they had accumulated over the years.

The whole idea of Christmas had brought nothing but tears this year. She'd agreed to do Santa's Thrift Shop because of the pressure from the townsfolk. Now she was glad she had. It would be the last one, and the warm memory would have to last her a lifetime.

When they got home, Cal made another pot of coffee while Giselle dragged out the Christmas gifts.

"Let's wrap!" she said.

"Music?"

"Yes."

Cal put on a Christmas CD, and the couple sat, cross-legged on the floor, wrapping gifts and sipping coffee. For a second, Giselle stopped and sighed. She'd never envisioned this scene. Instead, images of a cold and empty holiday spent alone with frozen food and audiobooks had squeezed her heart. In the past, memories of glorious Christmas celebrations with her parents had sustained her. But the last few years, the holiday had lost its meaning, until today.

She hummed along with her favorite tunes. "Are you going to sing along tonight?"

"You know I have no voice."

"So? Neither does anyone else."

"Have you met Stryker West? His voice is amazing."

"So what? I like your voice. Sing tonight."

Cal laughed. "You'll live to regret it."

Chapter Fourteen

When they finished, they loaded all the presents in the car and drove to Betty and Al's. The aroma of simmering chicken soup greeted Giselle, making her mouth water.

"Come in, come in," Betty said, pulling on their arms. "It's cold out there."

"Need a hand?" Al asked.

"There's more in the car," Cal replied.

Betty took Giselle aside. "I'm so glad you're staying the night. This has become a family tradition. Ever since Jane passed, Cal and Bobby have come here Christmas Eve and stayed over. Bobby likes being here crack of dawn to open his gifts."

"What about Jane's parents? Are they around?"

"Oh, dear." Betty's eyes wetted. "They were killed in a car accident. They didn't approve of Cal. Jane almost didn't marry him. But after they died, she married Cal to give Bobby a father. So sad they never met their grandson."

Giselle hugged Cal's mom.

The men tromped in and out, carrying a boatload of presents in shopping bags. Once they had stowed the gifts in a safe place, away from curious young eyes, they sat down at the table for a hardy lunch of Betty's secret recipe chicken soup, homemade bread, cheese, and ham. Giselle ate like she hadn't seen food in a week. She remembered Betty's cooking from the afternoons she had spent at Cal's house, munching on pies and cookies.

"This is delicious, Betty."

"I'll give you the recipe. Now you're gonna be family," the older woman said, beaming.

The heat of embarrassment went to her cheeks. Giselle couldn't figure out why it should make her uncomfortable.

"All I can say is, it's about damn time!" Al chuckled.

Giselle buttered a thick slice of white bread and looked around. The place hadn't changed since she'd last been there. Too many *tchotchkes* on the mantle and the end tables, overstuffed sofa and two chairs in floral chintz prints gave the room a welcoming, lived-in feeling. The big blaze in the fireplace warmed the living room.

The sofa invited her to tuck her legs under and snuggle back into its cushiony softness. She jumped up to help clear the table.

"Sit," Betty said, placing a restraining hand on her arm. "You're a guest. At least for a little while longer."

"I'll get it." Al rose from his chair. The men whisked away the dishes. Al loaded everything right into the dishwasher while Betty fussed over dessert.

"Let's move to the living room. Hate to let that fire go to waste," Betty said, bringing out a tall chocolate cake.

"Dad is the king of fires. Mine can't even compare," Cal said.

"Aw. Shucks," Al muttered.

"Don't overdo it. It'll go to his head," Betty said.

As the banter continued, Giselle cuddled a tiny bit closer to Cal sitting next to her and listened. The small Morrison family laughed and joked with each other, teasing, professing fake injured feelings and retaliating. She loved the phony insult one-upmanship they engaged in.

Without doing anything obvious, they drew her into the warmth of their loving circle. After an insult, one would turn to her and ask for approval of their snarky comeback. She nodded and laughed.

Like a piece of a jigsaw puzzle, Giselle fit in. They embraced her, without saying anything directly or making a fuss. She sensed the subtle acceptance of Al as he made fun of his son and solicited Giselle's approval. Or the way Betty bragged about her son then looked to Giselle to agree. Before she could analyze what was happening, it had happened.

Cal covered her hand with his and moved them to his knee. She belonged here, in this family. They'd saved a place for her in their hearts and dusted it off, opening to her when the time was right. Gratitude filled her, watering her eyes a bit before she blinked it back.

"What's for dinner tomorrow, Ma?" Cal rose from the sofa to fetch coffee.

"You just finished lunch, Calvin Morrison. And now you want to know about dinner?" Betty asked, her tone mocking.

Cal blushed. "I don't get to eat like this all the time. I want to enjoy the anticipation."

Betty slapped him on the shoulder then gave him a hug. "This boy. Gotta love him. He's my best audience, ya know?"

Giselle nodded. "Cal appreciates a good meal."

"So, Ma?"

"Okay, okay. All your favorites. Baked ham, scalloped potatoes, Caesar salad, Brussels sprouts…"

"And chocolate cake for dessert?" he finished.

"Well, yeah. And butterscotch pudding," Betty said then faced Giselle. "Al's favorite."

"Oh, I almost forgot! We have gingerbread cookies. Bobby's favorite. Al and I made them yesterday. I swear this man ate almost as many as he cut out!"

Betty asked Giselle to keep her company while she made mulled wine. Cal went to pick up Bobby at school.

"I had Cal put your things in his room. Is that all right? If it isn't, he can sleep on the sofa." Betty took down a bottle of wine from a tall cabinet.

Giselle detected a blush on Betty's face. "Yes, it's fine."

"Oh good. I figured. I mean when Cal said you'd be spending weekends there and all. I don't want to presume anything, But I thought—"

"It's okay, Betty. Don't worry. You did the right thing." She touched the older woman's shoulder. The look of relief on her face brought a smile to Giselle's.

"Come on, Giselle." Al slung a coat over his shoulders. "I gotta get more wood. Walk with me."

"Okay."

Grateful to have an easy exit, she took her coat off the hook in the front hall, donned her hat, and yanked on gloves. Al led the way. She fell in step with him.

"Cal said you want to sell the thrift shop," he began.

"Yes."

"Why?"

"A lot of reasons. I can't keep the place up. It needs work. I don't have the money or the ability now to handle that. And I need to work. Need to be useful and make some money."

"I see. Cal and I could spruce the place up, if you want. You'd never recognize it," he said.

"Thanks, Al. It's more than that. There's bookkeeping and other things I can't do now. I'd have to sell more than secondhand merchandise to afford the taxes."

"What would you do if you didn't run the thrift shop?"

"I have no idea. I'm trying to figure it out."

He patted her shoulder. "You'll come up with something. Have faith."

"Thanks."

Al echoed what Giselle thought her father would say. He'd be supportive. She needed that right now. Her life had been tossed around as if a tornado had hit it. Some things were good, some not so good, and some unknown. One minute, she'd be deliriously happy, the next, apprehensive. Scared of the future, afraid to expect happiness, she hung on, as if adrift in a boat on a stormy sea. Having faith she'd figure it out brought some semblance of peace.

When she and Al returned, Cal and Bobby were back. The boy sat for a glass of milk and a gingerbread cookie. When Giselle entered the house, he took a cookie off the plate and handed it to her.

"Have one, Mom," he said.

All motion stopped. The air thickened. Little shocks ran through Giselle.

"Thanks." She took the offering, biting her quivering lip.

"Daddy said I could call you that." He raised his big-eyed gaze to hers.

Betty teared up and left the room. Al's eyes widened.

"Okay?" Cal cocked an eyebrow at her.

"Yes. Perfect." She took a deep breath and ran her fingers through Bobby's hair.

"Don't muss it up. Santa will see it and think I've been bad," he said, desperately trying to comb it back in place with his fingers.

Giselle laughed. "Cal, gotta comb?"

He whipped one out of his back pocket and straightened out Bobby's hair. Giselle bent to kiss him. Betty returned, mopping her eyes.

"I never thought I'd hear Bobby say that," she mumbled.

Giselle squeezed her hand.

"What's for dinner?" Bobby asked.

"A chip off the old block." Al chuckled.

Bobby begged to stay up and see Santa, but Cal put his foot down. The boy was in bed and asleep by eight. The adults sipped mulled wine by the fire and talked about the gifts they got for the little boy.

Directing his conversation to Giselle, Al began, "We've tried not to spoil him, but when Jane died, Betty and I went overboard."

"Ya think? A trampoline for a three-year-old?" Cal piped up.

"But this year will be the biggest and the best," Betty said.

"How so? What did you guys get this time?" Cal groaned. "An airplane?"

Al laughed. "It's not our gift, Son. It's yours."

"Mine?" Cal's eyebrows shot up. "I didn't get him anything special."

"Oh, yes you did," Al said.

"You got him a new mother," Betty finished.

BETTY AND AL TURNED in at nine thirty, leaving Cal and Giselle to put out the fire and load the last few dishes into the washer. Giselle looked around. Cal's childhood room was small. The bed was a double, not a roomy queen like he had at his house.

Eyeing the mattress, Cal said, "I know it's not a queen, but it's only for one night."

"It's fine. We'll just have to sleep closer together," she said, grinning.

"Works for me."

They got undressed. Taking no chances, Giselle donned a flannel nightgown she'd bought for cold nights.

"Are you really gonna wear that thing to bed?" He fingered the material a moment before yanking his T-shirt over his head.

"Yep."

"Damn. This tiny bed and I were looking forward to...uh, some serious...well, whatever."

"Cuddling?"

"Yeah. That's not a guy word."

She laughed.

Cal pulled the covers down and, wearing only boxers, slid into bed. He patted the mattress next to him. "Hop in."

She eased in, and he covered them.

"I went to the doctor. I'm on the pill now. We're safe," she said.

"Really? Fantastic! How do I find you under all this?" He pushed and tugged at her gown.

"Here. Wait." She raised her hips and slid the nightgown up under her armpits. "Better?"

He closed his fingers over her rib cage. "Much better."

"I never thought we'd be spending the night in the same bed at your parents' house."

He laughed. "Me, neither. And unmarried but with their blessing."

"I guess things change," she said.

"My love for you hasn't changed."

"Only in between, you loved someone else."

"Can't you forget it? Are you going to remind me of Jane forever?"

"No. It's just... Well, I'm still getting used to believing this is real. You're real. And that you mean what you say."

Cal raised his knee. "Come over here."

She inched closer.

With his mouth a breath away from her ear, he spoke. "I will always love you. Always be here for you. As long as I'm alive, you will be my wife, my only love."

Her pulse slowed, her breathing evened. He raised his arm, and she scooted underneath. Running her palm along his pecs, she sighed. His skin was warm, the hair on his chest tickled her hand. She kissed him and trapped his leg between hers.

"Starting something?" he asked, his brows raised.

"Maybe."

He kissed her. "Quickie?"

"Maybe."

"Not real definite about this, are you? Let's see," he said, thrusting his hand between her legs. "Hmm, I'd say more than maybe."

He lowered his lips to her peak and stroked her with his fingers. Heat rose in Giselle's body. Desire surged through her. She wanted him.

"Cal. I..."

"Yeah. I know." He rolled over on top of her. She parted her legs, and, before she could take a breath, he was inside her. She moaned as he filled her. She settled her arms around him and dug her nails into his shoulders.

"Ow. Take it easy," he said.

"Sorry."

"Just kidding."

He reached around and hooked his hand under her knee, raising it to her chest. Her eyes drifted shut as every nerve ending jolted awake. Sensation buzzed up and down her body as he pumped into her. At the first squeak of the bed, they both burst into giggles. He slowed down, making the rising tension drop from light speed to a turtle crawl. His steady pace stoked her fire again until it raged.

With a grunt she attempted to stifle, she let the orgasm rule. Her hips pumped a rhythm all their own.

"Damn," he whispered, matching her beat for beat. Then he stopped, closed his mouth over a soft, fleshy part of her shoulder, and groaned into her body. His release took him.

He reached over to douse the light and brushed his lips against hers. Resting on his forearms, he let his fingers play with her hair.

"That was great," he whispered.

"Fantastic."

He eased out of her and turned onto his side. "Come up against me," he whispered.

She snuggled her butt into his hips as he wrapped an arm around her chest, his hand closing over her breast.

"I love you, Cal."

The two dozed. She rolled over, waking him.

"Zell."

"Hmm?" she asked, her voice heavy with sleep.

"Promise me," he mumbled.

"Hmm?" She stretched out her legs. "Promise you what?" she asked, more awake.

"Promise me you'll never leave me."

She couldn't tell if he was truly awake or talking in his sleep.

"Promise me you'll never leave me."

Shifting to her back, she opened her eyes and tried to make out his face in the dark. Instead, she ran a soft palm over his cheek, chin, and nose.

"I'll never leave you, Cal. I belong to you. I promise with all my heart," she whispered, stroking his face.

She felt his lips turn into a grin. "Good girl," he said then his breathing deepened and evened out.

She kissed him, eased her cheek onto the pillow, and closed her eyes. He'd never asked that before. Her heart swelled. No, she'd never leave him. Not in this lifetime.

A RAPID KNOCK WOKE Cal.

"He's been here!" The squeaky voice of a small boy came through the door.

"Come in, come in." Cal smoothed Giselle's nightgown down.

The door burst open, and a whirling dervish known as Bobby flew into the room.

"Who's been here?" Cal yawned.

"Santa! He left presents under the tree. Come on. Come on!" Bobby tugged on the blanket.

"Okay, okay. We're up. Are Grandma and Grandpa up yet?"

"No."

"You go wake them. Get Grandma started on breakfast. We'll be along in a minute," Cal said.

Bobby jumped on the bed and snuggled next to Giselle. She wrapped her arms around the boy and held him to her then kissed the top of his head. "Scoot, Bobby. I'm hungry. Aren't you?"

He nodded, slid off the bed, and ran out of the room.

"Christmas is his favorite day of the year. Can you tell?" Cal laughed.

She smiled as she shifted her legs over the side of the bed and pushed to her feet.

Cal eyed her as he pulled up the covers, his version of making the bed. "You don't need a robe with that thing. Damn, woman. It hides you completely. Can't even see where you are."

"That's the point." She scampered out the door, heading for the bathroom, toothbrush in hand.

He grabbed his robe off the hook on the back of his door and shrugged it on. One look in the mirror sent him straight for his comb.

"Dad! Mom!" hollered in a kind of wail met his ears.

Cal peeked out of the room and saw Giselle heading toward him.

"Gonna brush my teeth." He scampered down the hall.

Within a few minutes, Giselle and Cal joined his family at the Christmas tree.

"Coffee's ready." Betty pointed to a pot on the sideboard with all the fixings. "Thought we'd open a couple of gifts before breakfast."

"Good idea," Cal replied.

"Me, first!" Bobby reached for a package.

Cal fixed coffee for himself and Giselle then carried both to the sofa. The adults watched Bobby open his presents. Al scooped up bunches up wrapping paper and stuffed them in a big garbage bag. Cal snapped a few photos. Giselle couldn't believe how excited the boy got with each new toy.

In a whirlwind of joy, Bobby scattered farm animals, Legos, and Tinkertoys across the living room rug.

"Breakfast, Ma?" Cal asked.

"Coming up." She rose from her chair.

"Can I help?" Giselle asked.

"You and Cal can set the table. We'll eat in the kitchen. Dining room table is already set for dinner."

Betty made pancakes and sausage. Al whipped up mimosas for the adults, and the family chowed down. When they finished and cleaned up, they returned to the tree. Now it was time for the rest of the folks to exchange gifts.

Cal's big gift to Giselle was a talking pendant watch. She examined it closely. "It's beautiful."

"And it tells you the time. I tried it out. And already set it for the correct time." He took it from her and put it around her neck. She kissed him.

"A talking watch?" Bobby perked up, lifting his head from his focus on Legos. "Can I see?"

Everyone had to take a look and try it out.

"I want one, too," Bobby said.

"You don't need one. But I'll teach you how to tell time," Al said.

Giselle touched the watch and handed her gift to Cal. He opened the box to reveal a pocketknife with every gadget known to man, from a nail clipper to three different size blades to a tiny scissors.

"Unless you bought one in the past six years, I remember you talking about not having one and how much you wanted it," she said.

"This is fantastic!" He pulled out each item, including a small nail file. "It's got everything."

"That's what I said to the man at the counter. I said, 'I want one like a pizza, with everything.'"

He chuckled then kissed her. "Thank you."

"Are you gonna kiss after every present?" Bobby asked. "Yuck!"

Cal helped his father clean up while Giselle kept Betty company in the kitchen.

"I can do more, Betty. Please let me help."

"I've got this. I started preparing a couple of days ago. So everything is just about done. I made the cake early this morning. It's cool enough to ice now."

The women sipped coffee while Betty added buttercream frosting to the devil's food cake.

"Have you thought about a wedding?" Betty asked.

"A wedding? No." Giselle hadn't been completely truthful. She had thought about a wedding. But it only brought tears to her eyes. With both of her parents gone, a wedding would be melancholy, with a shadow of sadness that they couldn't be with her, hanging over it. She'd pushed the idea out of her mind.

"You should. I'd be glad to take you dress shopping."

"That seems like such a waste of money." Giselle added milk to her beverage.

"Every girl should be a real bride once in her life."

"Did you have a big white dress?"

"We couldn't afford a fancy one. My mother could sew anything, and she made me a gorgeous dress."

"How lovely."

"It's a shame your folks aren't here for this."

Giselle nodded, surprised that Betty had read her mind. "It's happening too fast." It was too painful to admit that Cal's mom had spoken the truth.

Betty patted her hand. "I know, sweetheart. You're not alone. Al and I'll help you. You're already like our daughter."

Bobby came running in. "Cake!"

"Not now. It's for after dinner. I think maybe you could use a little quiet time." Betty put down the bowl of icing.

"Let's go listen to one of those talking books I... I mean, *Santa* brought you," Giselle said, rising.

"How did Santa know I like talking books?" Bobby asked.

"Guess he just knows everything." She took the boy's hand.

GISELLE AND BOBBY FELL asleep on Cal's bed while listening to Winnie the Pooh. Lips gently brushed her cheek.

"Time for dinner," Cal whispered.

She stirred, jostled awake by the disappearing warmth from a small body next to hers.

"Dinner?" Bobby yawned.

"Yep. Smell the ham?" Cal asked.

The boy's eyes popped open. "Ham?"

Cal nodded.

"Oh boy!" Bobby slid out of bed and raced to the kitchen in his stockinged feet.

Giselle laughed. "Does he only know one speed—Indy 500?"

"Yep. Come on, sleepy lady. Ma's ham is the best."

Hunger gripped her guts. The sweet-and-savory aroma seduced her taste buds, and her mouth watered. She felt around for her shoes.

"You don't need shoes. Let's go." Cal laced his fingers with hers.

The couple strolled into the dining room. Betty helped Bobby fill his plate.

"Have a nice rest?" Al asked.

"Oh yes."

"Me, too," the boy piped up, heading to his place at the table.

"Oh, the sight of the two of you, cuddled together, sound asleep, warmed my heart," Betty said. "Here." She handed a plate to Giselle.

"Everything smells wonderful." Since her sight weakened, she paid more attention to smells and sounds.

"I'll tell you what everything is," Cal said, taking his own plate. "First, the ham, of course. Then sweet potatoes. Then garlic mashed potatoes. Brussels sprouts. Green bean casserole. Caesar salad. Oh, and Ma's special lime Jell-O mold."

"Oh my God. I can't eat all that!"

"Try a little bit of everything. Can I help you?" Betty asked.

"Give her a lot of ham, Ma. She likes ham," Cal said.

Giselle carried her food to her place at the table. The family said grace then dug in. Dinnertime conversation centered around the presents they'd exchanged.

"That's some tie you gave me, Cal." Al cut a piece of ham.

"It's about time you wore a bright color."

"But pink?"

"I can't believe you're intimidated by a color, Pop." Cal shook his head.

Betty went on about the cookbook Al got her and the subscription to a crafting magazine Cal gave her. "And the scarf! I'll be best-dressed at the next Women's Rotary meeting."

Giselle listened to the men banter back and forth, teasing each other. Bobby ate fast and finished first.

"Can I have cake now?" he asked.

"You'll have to wait until we've all finished eating," Cal said.

"That'll take forever!" the boy wailed.

The laughter of the adults did not cheer him. He stomped off to play with his toys. The meal ended soon after. Giselle helped clear while Al loaded the dishwasher and Betty put the food away. Cal checked on his son.

"We always like to watch a Christmas movie on this day while we have dessert. Would you like to select the movie? Do you have a favorite?" Betty asked Giselle.

"It doesn't matter to me. I can't see the television easily unless it's huge."

Betty covered her mouth with her hand. "Oh my God. I'm so sorry, Giselle. How insensitive of me."

"Don't be silly. There's no reason why you shouldn't watch a Christmas movie. I can hear it just fine."

Bobby came bounding in. "Can we listen to a talking book instead? I want to finish Winnie the Pooh."

"What a good idea, Bobby! Sure. I can knit while I listen, too."

Right after the book ended, Bobby fell asleep on the sofa.

"I think we should be heading home." Cal picked up his son.

"It's late. Cold. Why not stay one more night?" Al asked.

"Good idea," Giselle piped up. She hugged Al and Betty. "This is the best Christmas I've had in a very long time. Thank you so much."

"Glad you could be with us," Al said.

"May this be the first of many." Betty squeezed her forearm.

They settled Bobby in his room then returned to theirs. Once under the covers, Giselle cozied up to Cal. He tucked her into his shoulder.

"Well, what did you think of the Morrison Christmas?"

"It was wonderful. Storybook. And everyone gets along. No fighting. I wouldn't change a thing."

"Ma's a good cook."

"Not just cook. The cake. Oh my God!"

"Yeah. Her specialty. That cake and the ham."

"Everything was perfect. Thank you, Cal."

"Don't thank me. You're part of the family now."

At his words, goose bumps ran up her spine. She said a little prayer nothing would upset her blissful life.

She and Cal kissed good night and spooned. Giselle closed her eyes. Peace drifted through her, and sleep came easily.

Chapter Fifteen

Back in Cal's house, life calmed down, and they settled into a family routine. Cal's cell rang.

"Hi, Pop. What's up?"

"St. Boniface Church has some work for us. Seems to be warm enough to do a little tree trimming of the lower branches. We can save the higher stuff for April. What do you say?"

"Good. I hate sitting around the house."

"Getting those projects done?"

"Not fast enough. Are we starting today?"

"If you can."

"Sure."

The men synchronized their watches and agreed on a time to meet at the church. Cal packed his tools into his truck.

"What are your plans for today?"

"Thought I might make some chili for dinner. And then maybe get started cleaning out the thrift shop."

"You still planning to sell it?"

She nodded. "I have no choice."

"Everyone has choices, Zell."

"I can't run the place full-time because we don't have enough business to pay the taxes on the property. I'll lose money."

"I hate for you to sell it," he said, ignoring her reasoning.

"I know. I don't like it, either. Every time I go there, I feel my mother's presence."

"Maybe we can think of something before you find a buyer."

"Can you drop me there on your way today?"

"Sure."

They climbed into the truck. When they reached the thrift shop, Giselle got out and made her way up the three steps to the shop. Once she managed to unlock the door, the scent of stale gingerbread met her. She went in the back and took out a black, plastic garbage bag.

After an hour of sorting as best she could, she filled the bag with the oldest clothes, the ones she didn't think would sell, and sealed it up. Then she placed it on the tiny front porch. Plopping down in a chair, she hugged herself.

"I'm sorry, Mom. I can't keep it up," she said to the air.

Emotion gathered in her chest. Tears stung her eyes. Walking away from the thrift shop would be one of the hardest things she'd ever done. A sudden thirst gripped her. Only a few blocks from The Cozy Café, she wandered over.

"Hi, Giselle. How ya doin'?" Laura Dailey asked. "Take a seat any-where, hon."

The café was only half-full, so Giselle had her choice of tables. She sat next to the window overlooking Cedar Lake. It was a brighter spot and helped her vision.

"Whatcha havin'?" Laura asked, her pencil in hand.

"How about a ham and egg sandwich on a croissant?"

"You got it. Something to drink?"

"Earl Grey tea?"

"Milk and sugar or lemon?"

"Milk and sugar."

"Got it."

Giselle texted Cal to pick her up at the café instead of the thrift shop then headed for the ladies' room. When she came out, Laura was on her way with the food. She put it on the table but didn't leave.

"I'm sure sorry you're selling the thrift shop," Laura said.

"Me, too. Can't help it. Sales don't even cover the taxes."

"That's a shame. Maybe some of us could help. Give you a hand."

"I appreciate that. But I don't think there's anything to be done." Laura nodded and left.

Giselle tucked into her sandwich. When she finished, her cell rang. She didn't recognize the number but answered it anyway.

"Giselle?" asked a male voice with a heavy accent.

"Yes. Who's this?"

"Gunther. Gunther Weber. You can't have forgotten me already?"

Giselle stiffened. "No. I haven't forgotten you." *Not for lack of trying.*

"Good. I hope you don't hold our breakup against me?"

"What do you want?" She stopped to take a sip of her tea.

"This call is business, not personal. So, don't hang up. Okay?"

"Make it fast."

"Ooh. She bites."

"If you don't want me to hang up, then don't talk to me that way."

"I'm sorry. Really. Anyway, let me get to the point."

"Please do."

"Your work has been written up in magazines. The Bauers, your former employers, want to do a book. They want to put out an office design book. And they want to hire you to write it."

"What? You know I don't see well enough to use a keyboard."

"They know that. They say you can dictate it."

"Dictate a book?"

"Yes."

"That's insane."

"It's a work-for-hire, and they would pay twenty-five thousand American dollars to you."

Giselle paused.

"Think about it, Giselle. It's a lot of money. Maybe six months of work. Maybe even less. They would provide the stenographer to take down your words."

"What's the catch?" Wasn't there always a catch to a windfall?

"They want you to do it here."

"What?"

"Right. Come back to Germany. They'll provide a studio apartment."

"I could dictate to the computer."

"Maybe. But it won't have the inflections a person can add. Besides, there would be an editor there working with you as you write. Guiding you."

"This is crazy."

"Sounds like a good opportunity to me," Gunther said.

Thoughts swirled through Giselle's brain. "I don't want to go back to Germany."

"Okay, okay. We thought you'd say that. They said I could increase the offer. How about thirty-five thousand?"

"Thirty-five thousand American dollars?"

"Yep."

"I don't know. Go back to Germany?"

"Yep. Think about it. Sleep on it. I'll call you before New Year's, eh? Oh, Happy Christmas," Gunther said, and hung up the phone.

Giselle gripped her mug with both hands. A deep voice interrupted her thoughts.

"So, when are you going back to Germany?"

She turned to face Cal, standing in the doorway.

"HOW LONG HAVE YOU BEEN standing there, eavesdropping?" she asked.

"Long enough. And it's not eavesdropping when you're speaking in a public place." When she avoided his question, Cal's guts twisted.

"Coffee, Cal?" Laura said.

"No," he said, brushing her aside.

He wouldn't be sidetracked. He strode across the room in three steps and plopped down in the seat next to his fiancée.

"You haven't answered my question," he said, his voice husky as anger flashed through his chest.

"I'm not going to Germany."

"Didn't sound like you made that decision," Cal continued.

"Yet. The key word is 'yet.'"

"And that was your former fiancé calling?" He sensed red creeping up his neck.

"Gunther? Yes. So what? I can't stand him."

"You had a pretty civil conversation for hating the man."

"Actually, it wasn't that civil. Guess you didn't hear the beginning."

"Are you going to Germany?"

"No."

"Is that definite?"

"Can't I at least take an hour to think about the offer?"

"What are they offering?"

"A lot of money. It could make a big difference. We could put it into a college fund for Bobby."

He clenched his fist. "I don't give a damn about money. I do fine. I'll be able to send him to college without your help," he spit out.

Her head snapped back as if he'd hit her. "This is about us."

"Damn right it is. Can we talk at home?" Cal pushed to his feet. He grabbed Giselle's jacket and held it for her. She ripped it out of his grip and put it on by herself.

He dropped a few bills on the table, nodded to Laura, and opened the door for Giselle.

"Where's the car?"

"Third on the right." Jogging, he managed to get to the car first and open her door.

"Don't pull the gentleman act now. You've already blown it."

"You've got ice on your tongue."

"You put it there."

He started the car and pulled out onto the street. "What's this Germany thing all about?"

Giselle repeated what Gunther had told her. By the time she finished, they were in the driveway of Cal's house. She got out and stood, waiting for him. His keys jingled as he headed for the walk. She turned toward the street.

"Where are you going?" he asked.

"Home."

"This is home."

"That's your home, which you made very clear. I have my own home. Across the street." Her tone could freeze meat.

"Don't be like that. We need to talk." Cal had put his foot in it, letting his temper get the best of him. He had some backpedaling to do.

"Talk to yourself," she said, taking steps toward her house.

He sprinted to catch up. Grabbing her elbow, he stopped her. "Come on. I'm sorry. I was a little gruff."

"A little?" she asked, her eyebrows heading north.

"Okay, okay. A lot. The idea of you going back to Europe makes me crazy."

"That's your problem." She sniffed.

"No, that's our problem. Come on. Come on. Don't get all snooty with me."

"Now I'm snooty?" she asked, her voice rising several octaves.

Damn it, why did he keep putting his foot in it? Why couldn't he be nice, calm, rational? Trusting her still scared the crap out of him. Would this prove him right to hang back and protect his heart? Or was it already too late for that? He grabbed her upper arm.

"You know what I mean. Please, Zell. Come back to the house—our house."

"You're hurting me," she said.

He loosened his grip.

She narrowed her eyes but turned around. He snaked his arm around her waist, his step fell in with hers. Cal fished the keys from his pocket again and opened the door. He stood aside, letting her enter first.

"Coffee?" he called over his shoulder as he turned the lock.

"I'll make it."

Her voice sounded even. He let out a breath. Maybe he'd averted a major meltdown between them. He hung his coat on a hook and headed for the fridge. They bustled around the kitchen, preparing the hot beverage then came face-to-face at the table.

"It's a lot of money, Cal."

"I don't care. You'd be gone six months. Last time you went, things didn't go well."

"That was you, not me."

"That was both of us."

"This time would be different. We could get married before I went."

"No."

"No to the marriage?"

"No to Europe. Doesn't a promise mean anything to you?"

HER EYES WIDENED. HE had been awake when he made her promise never to leave him. She'd thought he'd been talking in his sleep. She'd promised and meant it, but the money...where could she earn that kind of money so fast? It was tempting. Did she want to go back? Nope. Did she want to see Gunther again? Definitely not. But she had to consider all three of them now that she was part of a family.

"You didn't answer my question."

"Of course, a promise means something to me. But this opportunity. To get so much money at one time?"

"You promised."

"I know."

"If you break that promise, it's finished between us. And for good. I can't go through this anymore, Giselle. Either you're committed to Bobby and me, or you're not."

"And six months would make a difference?"

"A promise is a promise. At least to me."

"Okay, then. It's decided. It's not like I wanted to go. I didn't."

"And now?"

"I'm not going."

Cal's brows knitted.

"You're not jumping for joy," she said.

"You sound pissed off."

"You don't want to talk it out."

"There's nothing to talk out. You made a promise, and I want you to keep it."

"I said I would." She pushed her chair out and went to the window. Why was she making such a fuss? She didn't want to go, hated Gunther, and needed to build her life here. Maybe because she didn't have her own life in Pine Grove yet? Maybe that was the problem? Or maybe Cal's insistence, his controlling attitude rubbed her the wrong way? It was one thing to love someone, and another to smother them, take charge of their every movement.

"You're doing it under duress." Cal followed her.

"You're pressing me."

"It's important." Cal added milk to his beverage.

"I know."

"So, what's the problem?"

She shrugged. "I don't know. I don't want to go. Didn't the minute he made the offer. But I wanted the chance to think about it. Weigh the pros and cons. Myself. Without pressure from you. I wanted it to be my decision."

He stared at his hands. "I'm sorry. I keep apologizing. I'm a klutz."

"No, you're a great man. You love me. I get that."

"I do. You, Bobby, you're my world," he said.

"And you're mine. That's why I don't want to go. Six months without you? I'd go crazy."

He sidled up next to her and leaned in for a kiss. "You belong to me, Giselle. Face it. Embrace it."

"I do. And you belong to me, Cal Morrison, and don't you forget it!" She poked him hard in the chest.

He laughed and pulled her to him. She melted into his arms, soothed by his scent and the warmth of his body. The bad news? Turning down so much money. The good news? Cal wanted her here instead of the cash.

She laughed to herself. Cal Morrison liked to be captain of the team. Controlling? Bullheaded? A touch arrogant? Those aspects of his personality hadn't changed. She could bank on his attitude, but could she count on his love?

When they broke, Cal cleared the table and set the mugs in the sink. "Well?"

"Well what?"

"Aren't you gonna call him?"

"Call who?"

"That asshole who offered you this dumbass job."

Anger heated inside her. "It's not a dumbass job."

"Okay, okay. Maybe it isn't. Aren't you going to tell him 'no'?"

After drying her hands, she threw down the dish towel. "I'll think about it. And do it when I'm ready!" Giselle stormed off, heading for the bedroom. She slammed the door.

Pacing by the window, she itched to give Cal a piece of her mind. Who did he think he was, telling her when to call Gunther? If he thought love meant ruling her life, bossing her around, he had another think coming!

She stopped pacing, listening for his knock on the door. But it didn't come. Where was he? The fact he didn't follow her in to apologize for the millionth time irked her even more. She waited and waited, but no sound came from the hall.

Then he burst into the room, scaring her to death. She jumped and fell backwards. Pushing to her feet before he could help her up, she yelled.

"What the hell was that?"

"If you think I'm gonna apologize for calling that asshole an asshole for calling my fiancée and trying to lure her back to Germany, you can forget it. And calling the job dumbass? Maybe it isn't, but I don't like it anyway."

"All this to *not* apologize?"

He folded his arms across his chest and gave one nod. As quickly as it entered her body, the anger drained. She collapsed in laughter and fell onto the bed.

"What are you laughing at?" he asked, his tone guarded.

"You! You're hilarious! You make no sense."

"Maybe. Maybe not. But you shouldn't laugh at me."

"I'm sorry, but I can't help it. You're funny. Sweet and funny."

"The sweet part is okay. What's funny?"

"You're so possessive. You're afraid of Gunther—who I can't stand. I truly hate his lying, double-dealing ass. And you think he could ever beat you out for my love. That's funny."

He unfolded his arms and gave forth a chuckle. "That is funny, isn't it?"

"Yep," she said, continuing to laugh.

Cal fell next to her on the bed. He crawled up to capture her face between his hands. "I love you, Giselle."

"And I love you, my stubborn, arrogant man."

"Am I stubborn and arrogant?"

"Maybe just a little," she said, pulling his head down so their lips met.

BUT THE AIR DIDN'T clear completely between them. Betty and Al invited them to dinner. Bobby played with toys he had stashed at Grandma and Grandpa's while the adults had cocktails and fixed dinner. Al took charge of the salad. Giselle peeled potatoes. Cal sipped a beer and hauled in wood for a fire while Betty checked the meat.

"Call Gunther yet?" Toting four logs, Cal brushed by Giselle on his way to the living room.

"Nope."

He stopped to face her. "Why not?"

"I've been busy. I have buyers coming to look at the thrift shop. I've been over there, cleaning. Then making dinner and doing stuff."

"Just an excuse," he said, continuing on his way.

When he returned to wash his hands, he shot a sharp glance at her. Giselle spoke up. "Stop telling me what to do. I'll call when I'm ready."

"When will that be? *Before the next millennium?*"

Betty and Al continued preparing food in silence. Giselle caught them exchanging glances once or twice.

"Leave it alone, Cal," she said.

"You're going, aren't you?"

"No!" She scraped a spud in anger. The peeler slipped and cut her hand. Cal was all over her, dragging her to the kitchen sink.

"Let me wash it off," he said.

She yanked her hand away. "I'll do it."

Al stepped aside, turning over the faucet to her. "Let me see that," he said, gently taking her hand. He cleaned the wound then led her to the bathroom for antiseptic and a Band-Aid. When they returned to the kitchen, Giselle sensed a hostile glare from Cal.

"Will you two knock it off?" Betty said, hands on her hips, her lips compressed into a frown.

Cal and Giselle faced her.

"You guys have been going at each other for days. Resolve this and move on. Geez. What happened to the man and woman who couldn't keep their hands off each other?"

"She's right, you know," Al piped up.

Their sniping wore Giselle down.

"I'm sorry," she said. "We'll stop. Won't we, Cal?"

He nodded and exited by the back door.

While they didn't exchange angry or sarcastic words, they simply clammed up, adding to the tension in the room. Bobby asked to take his meal in front of the television. Betty glared at her son then gave her grandson permission. Al carried the boy's plate and utensils into the den.

"Can't blame him for wanting to get away from you two. You're ruining a great meal," Betty said. "Even if I do say so myself."

"It is great. Thank you," Giselle said.

"We haven't said a word!" Cal whined.

"You don't have to. You could cut the tension between you two with a knife," Betty replied.

When dinner was over, Giselle and Cal left. Bobby fell asleep in the backseat. Cal carried him into his room, undressed him, and put him to bed.

Tense and exhausted, Giselle washed up and went to bed. Too keyed-up to sleep, she felt the mattress dip when Cal joined her. Being jostled as he got comfortable annoyed her.

"You done?"

"What do you mean?"

"Are you quite comfortable?" she asked.

"Yes. Thank you. Did I wake you?"

"You would have if I'd been asleep."

Cal reached over and ran his hand along her rump. "Hmm. Flannel. Guess it's good night."

"You got that right." She rolled away from him.

"Okay, okay. I can take a hint."

"Good."

"In case you change your mind."

"I won't." Giselle bit her lip. She'd never turned Cal down for sex before.

He sighed, rolling on his side, with his back to her. She swallowed. He sounded so weary. While she knew he was stubborn, she'd never seen him hold on to anger this long. And what about her? Shame filled her. She loved him. What was she doing? Sleep claimed her before she could change her mind.

When she awoke in the morning, Cal and Bobby were heading out the door. Bobby ran in for a goodbye kiss then took off to join his father. She dragged herself out of bed and washed up before he returned home.

"I've got tree work this morning. I called Mom and Dad. They're coming to take Bobby tonight. We've got to talk. That okay with you?"

She nodded. Then he was gone. No goodbye kiss, nothing. Her heart hung heavy. She hated to send him off to work without loving words and a kiss. But he'd dashed out the door too fast, obviously avoiding her.

Cal was right. They needed to talk. Would this stupid argument break them up? She shuddered to think of life without him. Did she need to stand her ground, be so tough and uncompromising? Not if the price of her pride was losing Cal. Tears started and wouldn't stop. She'd been almost there.

Twirling the engagement ring on her finger, Giselle faced herself in the mirror. An unhappy, tearstained countenance peered back. She'd been filled with joy, and now, dread, foreboding, afraid of what lay ahead.

"You're my daughter, but, Giselle, you can be one stubborn child." Her father's words, echoed in her head. Was she simply being unreasonable and difficult? Maybe. And maybe Cal was, too.

She dressed and tossed stew ingredients into the Crock-Pot for dinner. They'd need sustenance if they were going to talk it out. Silently, she blessed Betty for taking Bobby.

Betty and Al turned into the driveway with Cal's truck right behind them.

"I'll get your things, Bobby," Al said.

Betty stopped just inside the door. "Okay, you two. Get your coats and get in Cal's truck."

"What?" Cal asked.

"You heard me. Both of you. You and Giselle. Get in the truck," Betty repeated.

Al came out a few minutes later, holding Bobby's hand and carrying a small valise.

"We'll be home, Betty. Let me know how it goes," Al said then left, his eyes straight ahead and his grandson in tow.

"What's going on?" Giselle asked.

"This is an intervention. Get in the truck!" When Betty's hands met her generous hips, she meant business. "And I'm driving." Shoving Cal out of the way, she hoisted herself into the driver's seat. "Buckle up."

"Giselle got in the back, and Cal took shotgun.

"Where are we going, Ma?" Cal asked.

"You'll see."

Betty pulled into a parking lot and shut off the motor. "Follow me."

Cal and Giselle did as they were told.

"Where are we?" she whispered to Cal.

"City hall," he whispered back.

"City hall?".

"That's right." Betty headed for the front door.

She stopped in a quiet corner then faced them.

"This is an intervention. You two stubborn, impossible people have got to make a choice. Either you get married or call it quits. I'm here to see you patch up this stupid argument and tie the knot. Here. And. Now. Today."

"Isn't there a waiting period?" Cal asked.

"Your father spoke to the clerk and explained you'd already waited over six years and that ought to be long enough. He agreed. So, here." She waved a form in front of them. "This is guaranteed to be approved for an instant ceremony. Make up your minds. Do you love each other enough to spend the rest of your lives together, or are you going to be stupid and walk away?"

Silence filled the anteroom.

Giselle raised her gaze to Cal. He moved closer.

"I'm getting a cup of coffee. By the time I'm finished, you had better have made up your minds." Betty huffed off to a machine by a bench.

Cal put his arm around Giselle's shoulder and drew her closer. He bent his head to whisper in her ear. "If you really want to go to Germany...I mean, if it means that much...it's okay with me. I can't hold you here if you don't want to be held. I'll wait for you."

Breath caught in Giselle's throat. She reached out and fisted the lapel of his jacket. "Do you mean that?"

"You'll always belong to me, but only if you want to, Zell. I can't force you to marry me and stay here."

"But I want to."

"Only if you're sure."

"I am. I don't want the job."

"You sure?"

She nodded then fumbled around in her purse, seeking her phone.

"Can you help me? I want to redial Gunther." She handed him the phone. He flipped through other calls until he found the right one.

"You're sure?" he asked.

"Never been more sure of anything in my life."

"Okay, then." He pressed *dial* and handed the device back to her.

She held it to her ear. Gunther answered.

"Well, Liebeshen."

"Don't call me that," she snapped.

"Ouch. Okay. What's your decision?"

"I'm not taking the job. Don't call me again, Gunther. I'm getting married, and I don't want you or any work in Europe ever again."

"Wow. You sure?"

"Absolutely. Understood?"

"Oh yes. Wishing you a good life," he said.

"Goodbye," she said then ended the connection.

Before she could put away the phone, Cal grabbed her, engulfing her in a giant bear hug.

"Zell, you did it. You did. You're staying," he said, his voice thick with emotion.

"Of course. I love you, Cal. Always have. Always will."

Before she could utter another word, his mouth came down on hers in a hungry kiss. She flung her arms around his neck and held him tight. Tears stung the backs of her eyes. Love flowed through her veins. Oh, to be held by him, to kiss him—so damn good!

When they broke, she spoke up. "One more question."

"Shoot."

"Kids. I don't know if I can take care of a baby. If I can see well enough," she whispered, her voice trembling.

"A baby?"

"I want to have at least one child with you."

"At least?" Cal asked.

"Yep. Do you? We haven't discussed this."

"Of course, I want more kids. And with you? Perfect."

"But what about...?"

He put his finger over her lips. "We'll figure it out. Don't worry. We'll raise more great kids, like Bobby."

"Really?"

"Really. Now, is there anything else you want to know?"

"Nope. That's it," she replied.

A voice interrupted them. "So, are you ready for the ceremony?"

Cal let go and faced his mother. "Damn right we are. Aren't we, Zell?"

"Yes. We are."

Betty's face broke into a wide grin. "Thank God! Let's go."

The threesome entered the clerk's office. While Cal and Giselle bent over the form, filling in the blanks, a small voice rang out.

"Mommy! Daddy!"

Giselle looked up. Bobby raced over. Al joined them.

"Yes, when you two kissed, I called your dad. Thought Bobby might like to be here to watch his parents get married."

Cal chuckled. "Who knew you were such a romantic, Ma?"

"I did," Al piped up, grinning.

The clerk called their names. Cal laced his fingers with Giselle's as they stepped forward.

"For better or worse," she whispered.

"For better or worse," he responded.

"We are gathered here today to join this man and this woman in holy matrimony," the clerk began.

Betty pulled out a hanky. Cal tightened his grip on Giselle's hand.

Giselle smiled. *You belong to me, Cal Morrison.*

Epilogue

Giselle opened her eyes. The first thing she felt was the new wedding ring on the fourth finger of her left hand. She pulled it out from under the fluffy white down comforter and stared. Next, she raised her gaze to the giant windows facing Big Pines Mountain. She and Cal had taken a couple of days for a honeymoon at a local resort.

While she couldn't make out the details in the distance, she could see the light coming through the windows. Cal stirred. A masculine arm snaked over her bare waist and drew her to him.

"Good morning, Mrs. Morrison," he muttered, his speech thick with sleep.

"Betty?" She yanked the covers over her naked breasts.

He laughed. "No. You!"

"Oh! Yeah. I guess I am Mrs. Morrison now."

"You are. Sounds good to me." He nibbled on her shoulder.

They had made love four times the night before. There was a bit of soreness between her legs. She didn't object. A woman well-loved didn't mind being a touch sensitive.

"Husband," she muttered to herself.

He raised his head. "You rang?"

"Oh God. Is that all I have to do to get your attention?"

"Damn right." Cal lay back down.

She rolled over, cuddling into him. He splayed his fingers across her rump.

"Last night was the best night of my life," he muttered.

"Me, too."

Bobby was being spoiled at Betty and Al's, so the newlyweds had time to themselves.

"Do we have to get up?" she moaned.

"Nope." He snatched his watch from the bedside table. "Hmm. It's nine. Breakfast is coming at ten. Gives us time for a shower."

"Together?"

"What's your pleasure, wife?"

"Together," she said, giggling into his pecs.

Cal threw the covers off and leaped up out of bed. "Last one in the bathroom's a rotten egg."

Giselle swiveled and set her feet to the floor. Cal was way ahead. All she could do was melt on the floor in a puddle of laughter and bedsheets. He returned to rescue her, lifting her in his arms and putting her down in the shower.

The water was the right temperature. Cal stepped in, sticking his head under the spray. The lovers soaped each other up then made love. Cal hoisted her legs up, bracing her against the wall of the shower as he lowered her onto his stiff shaft.

Giselle had never made love like this before. She gave him control as he eased her up and down. Tension tightened inside. He nuzzled her neck, and she raked his back with her nails.

The orgasm grew, coiling, spiraling higher and higher. When he increased the pace, it burst forth, sending warmth all the way to her toes. He followed shortly after, standing still, burying his face in her neck.

When they were dressed and fed, Cal spoke up. "Let's go for a ride."

"A ride?"

"Sure. Why not? Some folks still have their Christmas lights up," he said.

"Even though it's the New Year?"

"Yeah. Stretching the season."

"Okay. Why not?"

"I thought we could stop for a burger at Homer's. If we can get a table by the fire."

"Sounds wonderful." She raised up on tiptoe to brush his lips with hers.

Hand in hand, the newlyweds headed outside. Cal opened the door to his truck for his wife.

When they pulled into Homer's parking lot. Cal's phone rang.

"You go in. I'll be in in a minute. Tree stuff," he said, opening the restaurant door for her.

"Okay."

"Ah, Giselle! Cal said you'd be by. I have a table by the fire for you." Homer ushered her to her seat then placed two menus on the table. "Mulled cider or mulled wine?"

"Oh, mulled cider sounds perfect."

"It's cold out today," Homer said.

"And we'll take our usual," Giselle said.

"Hmm. Okay. Two cheeseburgers, one medium and one well-done, right?"

"Right."

"Fries?"

"Yes."

"Coming right up."

She turned to the fire and stretched out her hands to warm. Bringing her finger up close to her eyes, she could make out her glittery diamond wedding band all in white gold. They'd bought it after the ceremony at city hall. For the ceremony's ring exchange, Cal's parents had let them use their rings.

"We've been married thirty-five years. Might bring you luck," Al had said, pulling his ring off and handing it to Giselle.

The flames kept a steady heat flowing toward her. She couldn't stop grinning. They'd done it, actually done it. Gotten married. No fanfare, no white dress, no tuxedo, just the county clerk, Betty and Al, Bobby, a fancy lunch, and poof—she was Mrs. Cal Morrison.

The fuss of a wedding would have simply been more of a challenge to her limited eyesight and a reminder of her departed parents. She didn't need all the little touches that went with the event. All she needed was Cal and the ceremony. And now she had what she wanted. Satisfaction flowed through her.

Thinking back to their wedding night gave her sexy shivers. Talk about an enthusiastic, inventive lover, Cal Morrison took the cake. Memories of their love that night got her engine revving. The man knew how to love a woman.

She had to come back to Earth after the marriage ceremony and face her future. The question about a career still nagged, yet she had no answer. Biting her lip, she admitted to herself she couldn't ignore those issues much longer. Giselle Davenport Morrison had to find something to do with her life besides being a wife and mother.

A gust of cold air interrupted her thoughts. Cal approached the table.

"Sorry about that."

"Everything okay?"

"Right on schedule."

"I ordered for us. Want to try the mulled cider?" she asked.

"Rather have a beer if you don't mind."

Homer brought their food with the brew. Giselle took a big bite of her burger.

"What do we need to fix in the house to make it safer for you?" Cal popped a French fry into his mouth.

Giselle mentioned the bathroom and the garage. They discussed how to handle making sure Bobby's toys were put away.

"I want to sell my house. We don't need it," she said.

"Let's crunch some numbers and see if we could make more renting it out. Dad and I can do any repairs and painting and stuff. Might be a nice steady income. Especially in the winter when my work slows down," Cal said.

"Good idea."

They finished lunch by sharing a piece of chocolate layer cake. Giselle decided to wait before bringing up her work. Now that they were married, there'd be plenty of time to talk about a job for her later.

When they got back in the truck, Cal suggested another stop. "Let's swing by the thrift shop."

"Okay. I hope no one has vandalized the place. I haven't been by in days."

Cal didn't respond. Giselle couldn't make out all the shapes and shadows, but it appeared there were cars in the parking lot. How could that be? The place was closed.

"Are those cars?" she asked, peering out the side window.

"Could be." Cal pulled into the lot and parked. "Come on. Let's go in." He helped her down then escorted her to the front door.

"Let's go in the side," she said.

"No, no. The front door," he said.

"The front door? Why?"

"You'll see."

When he opened the door, people popped up and yelled, "Surprise!"

Giselle jumped, staggering backwards, but Cal caught her before she went down.

"What the hell?"

"Look, Giselle. We've changed the shop," Jory said. "It's a craft shop now."

Giselle examined each shelf and table. She stared hard at the walls. They were a bright, clean white. She inhaled the smell of fresh paint. One table held crocheted blankets and throws. Another held handmade baby clothes. A macramé planter holder hung from the ceiling. A shelf held a famous brand of doll with basket after basket of handmade doll clothes.

Hand-sewn dresses hung on a rack. Everything from shifts to evening wear filled the space.

On the wall hung a spectacular quilt. There were even vases of artificial flowers fashioned by Pine Grove residents. The chairs were painted joyful colors, like orange and pink. The dull floor had been refinished. The store sparkled.

She tugged on Cal's sleeve. "What is this?"

He drew her close. "Your Pine Grove friends and neighbors wanted to give you a reason to keep the thrift shop. So, they turned it into a consignment shop. A place where you can sell handmade stuff by the folks in town."

"Really?"

"Yep. Then you won't have to lay out money for inventory. You can split the sales price fifty-fifty."

"Did you do this, Cal?"

"Dad and I contributed. We remodeled the place. But Laura Dailey and Jory and Mindy got people together. Who knew so many people in Pine Grove were that handy?"

"I guess they spent winter doing inside things," Giselle said.

"My husband, Barney, does woodworking in the winter. We've got a couple of his pieces here. Wooden cutting boards and trivets," Laura said.

"This is amazing. The place is full," Giselle said.

"And you should see the back room! Cal and Al built great storage so you can keep things from getting wrecked by bugs and dampness," Mindy added.

"And the sign. You have to see the sign," Jess Lennox said.

They shuffled out the front, and Giselle fished a small pair of binoculars from her purse.

There it was, in all its colorful glory: Giselle's Crafty Things. Turquoise blue on a white background.

"Who did the sign?"

"I did," Cal said.

"It's beautiful," Giselle said, perusing each letter with her binocs.

"Do you like it?" Jess asked.

"Please, say you'll run it and not sell," Jory pleaded.

"If you do run this place, Stryker will call his publicist and get you some publicity in New York publications. That should help sales."

"I'll keep the books for you," Mindy said.

"I'll do the computer work," Chris, the chauffeur, piped up.

Emotion choked Giselle. "You all did this for me?" Tears flooded her eyes.

"For you, and Pine Grove," Laura Dailey said. "Now we can have Santa's Thrift Shop every year."

Giselle went inside and plopped down on a chair. Everything looked and smelled so fresh and clean. They had transformed the dingy old thrift shop into a bright, light, inviting place.

"So, when you said you had tree work, you were really here?"

"Guilty. But it was only a little white lie," Cal said, holding his hands up. "So, what do you say?"

"Hmm. What can I say but a huge 'thank you' to everyone? Of course, I'll run the shop. It's already amazing. What a beautiful place to spend my days."

A cheer went up from the small crowd. People chatted and ate fresh scones donated for the opening by Laura Dailey.

"There's more stuff in bags in the back, too," Jory said.

Giselle rose to her feet. "This is the most wonderful gift in the world."

Cal chuckled. "You have friends."

"Ya think? Such fantastic people."

"I guess you could say that you belong to me, and to Pine Grove, Mrs. Morrison," Cal said, planting a quick kiss on her lips.

She grinned. "I guess you could."

****THE END****

If you enjoyed this book, please be kind and leave a short review. Thank you. Watch Pine for Flint's story, coming next to Pine Grove.

Have you read the first three books?

Books by Jean C. Joachim

<u>ECHOES OF THE HEART</u>
HEATHER & MIKE: THE ONE THAT GOT AWAY
SANDY & RAFE: SECOND PLACE HEART
LIZ & NICK: NO REGRETS
PAIGE & BILL: ONE FINE DAY
ANTHOLOGY
<u>HOCKEY</u>
THE FINAL SLAPSHOT
<u>BOTTOM OF THE NINTH</u>
DAN ALEXANDER, PITCHER
MATT JACKSON, CATCHER
JAKE LAWRENCE, THIRD BASEMAN
NAT OWEN, FIRST BASE
BOBBY HERNANDEZ, SECOND BASE
SKIP QUINCY, SHORT STOP
EXTRA INNINGS
<u>FIRST & TEN SERIES</u>
GRIFF MONTGOMERY, QUARTERBACK
BUDDY CARRUTHERS, WIDE RECEIVER
PETE SEBASTIAN, COACH
DEVON DRAKE, CORNERBACK
SLY "BULLHORN" BRODSKY, OFFENSIVE LINE
AL "TRUNK" MAHONEY, DEFENSIVE LINE

HARLEY BRENNAN, RUNNING BACK
OVERTIME, THE FINAL TOUCHDOWN
A KING'S CHRISTMAS
<u>THE MANHATTAN DINNER CLUB</u>
RESCUE MY HEART
SEDUCING HIS HEART
SHINE YOUR LOVE ON ME
TO LOVE OR NOT TO LOVE
<u>HOLLYWOOD HEARTS SERIES</u>
IF I LOVED YOU
RED CARPET ROMANCE
MEMORIES OF LOVE
MOVIE LOVERS
LOVE'S LAST CHANCE
LOVERS & LIARS
His Leading Lady (Series Starter)
<u>NOW AND FOREVER SERIES</u>
NOW AND FOREVER 1, A LOVE STORY
NOW AND FOREVER 2, THE BOOK OF DANNY
NOW AND FOREVER 3, BLIND LOVE
NOW AND FOREVER 4, THE RENOVATED HEART
NOW AND FOREVER 5, LOVE'S JOURNEY
NOW AND FOREVER, CALLIE'S STORY (prequel)
<u>MOONLIGHT SERIES</u>
SUNNY DAYS, MOONLIT NIGHTS
APRIL'S KISS IN THE MOONLIGHT
UNDER THE MIDNIGHT MOON
MOONLIGHT & ROSES (prequel)
<u>LOST & FOUND SERIES</u>
LOVE, LOST AND FOUND
DANGEROUS LOVE, LOST AND FOUND
<u>NEW YORK NIGHTS NOVELS</u>

THE MARRIAGE LIST
THE LOVE LIST
THE DATING LIST
<u>PINE GROVE SERIES</u>
UNPREDICTABLE LOVE
BREAK MY HEART
RENOVATING THE BILLIONAIRE
<u>SHORT STORIES</u>
SWEET LOVE REMEMBERED
TUFFER'S CHRISTMAS WISH
THE HOUSE-SITTER'S CHRISTMAS

About the Author

Jean Joachim is a USA Today best-selling, award-winning, international romance fiction author, with books hitting the Amazon Top 100 list since 2012. She writes contemporary romance, which includes sports romance and romantic suspense.

Liz & Nick: One Fine Day won second place in the erotic romance category of the Oklahoma Romance Writers of America's 2018 International Digital Awards.

Dangerous Love Lost & Found, First Place winner in the 2015 Oklahoma Romance Writers of America, International Digital Award contest. *The Renovated Heart* won Best Novel of the Year from Love Romances Café. *Lovers & Liars* was a RomCon finalist in 2013. And *The Marriage List* tied for third place as Best Contemporary Romance from the Gulf Coast RWA.

To Love or Not to Love tied for second place in the 2014 New England Chapter of Romance Writers of America Reader's Choice contest.

She was chosen Author of the Year in 2012 by the New York City chapter of RWA.

Married and the mother of two sons, Jean lives in New York City. Early in the morning, you'll find her at her computer, writing, with a cup of tea, and a secret stash of black licorice.

Jean has 57 books, novellas and short stories published. Find them here:

http://www.jeanjoachimbooks.com. Chat with Jean in her Facebook group, JJ's Book Buddies. Join here: https://www.facebook.com/groups/489790604419710/

www.ingramcontent.com/pod-product-compliance
Lightning Source LLC
Chambersburg PA
CBHW061618100726
47898CB00002B/711